Madman's Bend

Madman's Bend

ARTHUR UPFIELD

The American Reprint Company

To the Reader

It is our pleasure to keep available uncommon titles and to this end, at the time of publication, we have used the best available sources. To aid catalogers and collectors, this title is printed in an edition limited to 80 copies. It has been manufactured in the United States to American Library Association standards on permanent, durable, acid-free paper. ———— **Enjoy!**

Reprinted 1976 by Special Arrangement

International Standard Book Number 0-89190-552-9

To order contact
AMERICAN REPRINT COMPANY, a division of
American Reprint Co./Rivercity Press
Box 1200
Mattituck, New York 11952

Contents

Madman's Bend

Chapter One

Axe and Bullet

The girl sat in a rocking-chair, and on the end of the table beside her lay a ·32 Winchester repeating rifle. Four yards separated her from the rear door of the large living-room and, like the front door and all the windows, that door was bolted.

The house was built on a high, level spur stabbing at the Darling River, and it nestled against a wide arc of red-gums. A cold wind blowing hard through the night from the far-distant Southern Highlands complained angrily at the obstructing gums, preventing the girl from hearing what she listened for – the arrival of a utility driven by her stepfather.

She was not quite nineteen, physically strong, her body filling her poplin blouse and man's trousers and making them appear too small for her. Beneath the broad forehead the dark eyes seldom blinked in the lamplight, and the wide mouth maintained its signal of determined purpose. The lamplight occasionally gleamed on her dark hair, and pitilessly revealed the ravages of sun and wind on her complexion. Hard work had roughened her hands.

From an inner room a woman moaned and then called, 'Jill! Give me more aspirin.'

Jill Ma   .. turned up the wick of the lamp on the chest of drawers, where stood a jug of water, a bottle of aspirin, and salves. The woman's eyes were bandaged; the girl had to raise her on the bed and push the tablets gently between her lacerated lips.

'Still hurting, dear?' she asked compassionately, and after the woman had taken a little of the water she added, 'Just try to sleep.'

Her mother sighed as the girl lowered her to the pillow, and said, 'It's mostly my ribs where he kicked me. And my eyes and nose feel like hot irons. But don't take on, Jill. I'll be better presently. I'm sure I will.'

'If you're not by morning I'm ringing the policeman. You and I have reached the limit, and we'll have no more of it.'

'We mustn't,' protested the woman. 'I'll be better in the morning, and then we'll talk to your father. He'll have to mend his ways, and stop his drinking. You must never call Constable Lucas. We can't have a scandal. I've made my bed and must lie on it.'

The girl checked herself from vigorously denying that William Lush was her father, saying instead, 'All right, dear. We'll wait till the morning. Now just try to rest, just try.'

Mrs Lush sighed again, and, having turned down the wick of the lamp, her daughter stood awhile by the chest of drawers before returning to her rocking-chair and making a cigarette with expert fingers. The old American clock on the mantel above the range bonged once. It was half past eleven. Her 'father' should not be long now. He was a careful driver; in fact, much more careful when drunk than when sober. He would certainly be drunk when he left White

2

Bend to drive home through the cold of the windy mid-winter night, and in him all the slights would be bottled tight to be poured out on his wife. Yes, a careful man, one who minded his p's and q's in company, but without inhibitions when with those he dominated.

Jill Madden had been out that afternoon mustering sheep into a paddock farther from the river, which was expected to flood within a week. Returning home at about five, she had found her mother on the living-room floor, badly injured and shocked. Not delaying to investigate causes, she had lifted her mother into the bedroom, undressed her and tended the multiple injuries with the bush aids to hand. When the victim of brutal assault was quieter, the girl had learned that her stepfather had wanted a cheque from his wife and had gone berserk when she refused.

The history of this small pastoral property was not uncommon. Forty thousand acres had been taken from a very large leasehold and transferred to Edward Madden by the Western Land Board under the Closer Settlement Act. Madden had himself built his house on the spur of higher ground on the west side of the Darling River, and here Jill had been born. Madden had died when the girl was sixteen years old. During the last year of his life he had been a semi-invalid, and Jill had come home from boarding-school to help him and take the place of a hired hand. After his death Mrs Madden, compelled to hire a man, had engaged William Lush, an itinerant stockman down from Queensland. The following year she had married him. A month after the marriage Lush had revealed his nature, and life at Madden's Selection had rapidly deteriorated.

Lush had asked his wife for a cheque for three hundred pounds with which to settle debts incurred at the small township of White Bend. When she had refused because her account at the bank would have been unable to meet it, he had proceeded to punch her, knock her to the floor and kick her. He had then driven off to the township, twenty-four miles downriver.

The attack had been but one of a series, and the worst. Fear, plus her mother's aversion to scandal, had so far prevented Jill from complaining to the police or to the people at the homestead of Mira Station on the far side of the river; but tonight fear was subdued by desperation, and desperation sired determination to counter violence with violence. It was, of course, impossible to predict accurately the time of her stepfather's return. Jill knew that he had little cash. He could get credit at the hotel, but it would be limited, and as Lush was the type who must keep up a bold front he would certainly leave when the hotel closed at ten o'clock. It was his habit when drunk to drive at not more than ten miles an hour along the dirt track. Too bad he didn't drive at sixty and break his neck, Jill Madden thought.

The hundred-year-old American clock, infinitely more reliable than the modern product, whirred and bonged the midnight hour. The vibrations died, and the fury outside again clamped itself about the house. The girl reached for the rifle and again checked the cartridge in the breech and the magazine. She was icily resolute to defend her mother and herself.

One of the two dogs, chained to kennels built of old iron, barked, and Jill thought of the lambs and the enemy foxes, and then of the shearing due to be con-

4

tracted out next month. She recalled Ray Cosgrove saying he wanted her to marry him, then thought of Ray's mother, who owned Mira Station. Mrs Cosgrove would certainly forbid anything of the kind, and for that she couldn't be blamed. She was wealthy, and Ray was like a blazing lighthouse on her horizon. The thought of his marrying the stepdaughter of the lisping, drunken Lush would give Mrs Cosgrove a heart attack.

The dog barked again. The sound seemed far away and beyond the noise created by the wind through the trees and the worried-loose shed roofs. It was not unusual in winter months for the wind to blow night and day for a week, with never a cloud to mask the sun or dim the diamond stars.

The handle of the door was twisted and then the door was shaken.

The girl's left hand flew to her mouth to prevent herself from crying out, then dropped to grip the rifle. The hand about the stock slid over for the finger to curve about the trigger.

A boot thudded against the door, and her stepfather shouted, 'Open up, there! What the hell! Let me in, you bitch.'

'Go and sleep in the woolshed,' Jill said. 'Keep away from here.'

'What's that you said?' shouted Lush, and Jill repeated it.

'Doss in the woolshed?' he yelled. 'Doss—' A river of filth streamed through the plain wall-board door.

When it dried up the girl could hear nothing, until her mother wailed and then called out, 'What is it, Jill? Who's that outside? I didn't hear the utility.'

'Stay quiet, Mother. I'll deal with this.'

The man must have had an ear to the keyhole.

' "Stay quiet," she says! Gimme an axe. I want an axe.' Lush pounded on the door with boot and fist. The dogs barked furiously, and presently the phrase 'Gimme an axe' was continuously repeated in dwindling volume, indicating that Lush had gone for the wood-heap axe.

'Was that William?' asked Mrs Lush, leaning weakly against the frame of the bedroom doorway. Her bandaged head made her look grotesque, the bandage disarrayed to permit her to see with bloodshot eyes. Then: 'What are you doing with that rifle, child?'

'I'm going to keep him out, now and for always. I'm going to frighten him out.'

'Then be careful, be careful! Oh God! What have we come to?'

The girl stood, aiming the rifle at the door from her hip.

Lush returned, to kick at the door and yell: 'Now, you in there! I'm coming in, see? You let me in or I axe my way in, and if I have to do that you'll get worse than you ever got. And you too, Jill. I'll start on you good and proper, my oath I will.'

The girl aimed the rifle at the ceiling, and fired.

'Get away from that door,' she shouted. 'Get away if you're sober enough to understand. I'll fix you if you don't.'

'You'll fix me! What a laugh!'

The axe smashed at the door. The edge of the blade showed through and was withdrawn for another blow. The girl worked the lever of the rifle to discharge the empty shell and force another cartridge into the breech. The next blow brought the axe-head right

6

through the wood hard against the lock. The girl aimed from the shoulder and fired.

The axe remained in the door. Both dogs were barking, and they seemed much nearer in the momentary lull of the wind. The clock bonged once. The wind came again to thrash the gums along the river, and Mrs Lush screamed:

'You've shot him, Jill! You've shot him!'

Chapter Two

A Pair of Gossips

The township of White Bend stopped growing in 1920. The hotel, the post-office and the police station, one bank and one general store serve the few inhabitants and the surrounding sheep and cattle stations. Built on high ground on the west bank of the Darling, the remains of its early prosperity may still be seen in the rotting wharf and the wind-wrecked shed.

Constable John Lucas thought highly of White Bend. It was his first station, his wife was a local girl, and he loved the river at first sight. Still in his early thirties, athletic and interested in everything and everyone, he considered the job of conveying Detective Inspector Bonaparte up-river to Bourke a very pleasant chore. There was no obsequiousness in his manner, nor any sign of superiority due to Bonaparte's mixed ancestry.

Lucas had heard of Bonaparte at rare intervals, but had not known that he was in his territory until a station manager telephoned to ask if he could convey the Inspector to Bourke and the air service. Accordingly, having contacted his superior at Bourke, he left White Bend with Bonaparte shortly after noon on 19 July.

A Pair of Gossips

The River Darling is unique on several counts. Unlike the Murray, of which it is a tributary, it has character and atmosphere. The land it spans is flat. Though it runs roughly six hundred miles from Walgett to Wentworth at its junction with the Murray, the Darling so twists and turns that its over-all course is something like eighteen hundred miles. Save at the major bends the channel is steeply banked as though fashioned by men with gigantic ditching machinery, and the banks are of the same gradient, the same width apart, and the same height from Wentworth to Bourke. Along all its course the river is shaded and sheltered from the summer sun and the winter winds by massive red-gums forming an almost unbroken avenue. Along this river men have found a strange peace of mind, strange in quality and duration, and they have heard siren voices calling them back no matter how long they have been absent or how distant they may be.

The road from Wilcannia to Bourke follows the west bank of the Darling, but, because of the river's many twists, touches it only at the major bends, these bends being sometimes ten or a dozen miles apart. The land outside almost all the major bends is higher than average, and, since it gives height above flood level and a permanent water supply from the great hole excavated by the river in flood, it is favoured as a site for homesteads.

'You know, I've often thought that when I retire I'll build a house beside this river,' remarked the man known to many merely as Bony.

'Might come to it myself one day,' declared the policeman, his fair hair whipped by the strong north-east wind, his grey eyes alight. 'Plenty of fishing and

9

shooting. No wonder the old pensioners build themselves shacks a mile or less from a township. Who the heck would want to live in a city?'

'Difficult to understand why anyone should,' responded Bony, the wind making his dark-blue eyes small. 'Car coming,' he added.

'Mail, probably,' said the policeman. Two minutes later he nodded to the driver of the heavy car and was given a wave by a youth with flaming red hair. 'Leaves Bourke at eight, and due at White Bend at one. Faster than the old days with the Cobb & Co. coaches. You remember them? Before my time.'

'No,' replied Bony. 'The change to motors occurred about the time I was first looking at Australia.'

When they passed the tip of a major bend he was able to look down at the great water-filled hole and along the bed of the river, down which a tiny stream meandered to the next hole.

'When did the river stop running?'

'Eleven months back,' replied Lucas. 'But it's going to run again soon – and how, from all reports! Going to run a banker. The first of it is well past Bourke, or was at six o'clock last night. Give it a week and this road'll be out. Funny!'

'What is?'

'Twenty inches of rain in south central Queensland in one month, and not enough to fill a billycan down here. We missed the autumn rains, and had nothing so far this winter.'

They passed a prosperous homestead built at a bend. This, Lucas said, was called Murrimundi; like Mira, up-river on its far side, it had been deprived of three-quarters of its original area by the Lands Department. It was eight miles to the next bend, the track winding across monotonous dun-coloured flats. And at this next bend they found an abandoned utility.

'Belongs to a feller named Lush,' remarked Lucas, stopping to alight. 'Has a place up-river by half a mile.' Leaning into the cabin of the utility, he switched on the ignition. 'Run out of petrol, and walked the rest. In town last night till the pub shut. Then too drunk to check.'

'And too much of a hangover to fetch gas this morning,' Bony added.

Lucas agreed, and began to fill a pipe. Bony turned to the river to gaze beyond the high cliff over the usual deep, water-filled hole, and then along the straight, dry course for almost a mile, where the river turned southward. There, above a similar cliff-faced bend, he could see the roofs of Mira Station.

'Fine house there,' Lucas told him. 'You can't see it because it lies to the left, behind the gums. Began as a million-acre property carrying eighty thousand sheep through good years and bad. Now all that's left to the homestead is a hundred and forty thousand acres and about twenty thousand sheep. It'd do me, though, any time they'd like to make a present of it.'

Set on legs near by stood the Mira mail-box. Lucas casually glanced inside it and observed that someone had already collected the mail. He looked inside a second and smaller box, and from it took a bag bearing a label marked with the word *Madden*.

'May as well take it on,' he decided. 'I've no time for Lush, but the women are good – too damn good for him.'

On the far side of the bend the track forked; Lucas took the right, which followed the retreating river to a group of buildings hard against the red-gum avenue. The house was small and dwarfed by the shearing-shed. It needed paint, and the removal of old iron and other rubbish would have improved it still more.

Constable Lucas stopped his car a few yards from the closed door. He was about to knock when a girl, accompanied by two dogs, came out of the shearing-shed. She was wearing jeans and riding-boots, and Bony noted how she placed her feet like a man accustomed to horses. Lucas returned to stand by his car and wait for her.

She said, a little breathlessly, 'Good afternoon, Mr Lucas. I didn't want you to knock because Mother is poorly and lying down.' From the mail-bag he carried she glanced at Bony, still seated in the car, and then ordered the dogs to be gone.

'Oh! Sorry to hear about Mrs Lush, Jill,' Lucas said, proffering the bag. 'I brought this along in case your stepfather was busy. We're running up to Bourke, and I'll be back tonight. Anything I can get for Mrs Lush?'

'No. No, I don't think so, thank you. Bill Lush isn't here. I was going for the mail later. Thanks for bringing it.'

'That's all right, Jill.' Constable Lucas smiled. Bill still suffering, I suppose.'

'I wouldn't know,' the girl said stiffly. 'Haven't seen him since he went to town, and don't want to.'

'Well, he got home as far as the mail-box. Ran out of petrol.'

Bony could see the frown narrowing the girl's fine dark eyebrows. The sunlight glinted on her dark brown hair, and on the silver marcasite brooch fastened to her rough drill tunic.

Probably cleared away into a cubby-hole somewhere with a supply of booze he brought out,' she said bitterly. 'Wouldn't be the first time, Mr Lucas. You know him. Gets so he can't bear himself, let alone us. Why don't you lock him up when he's drunk? He wouldn't be leaving town sober.'

'Never known him to,' admitted the policeman, adding ruefully, 'still, I can't lock him up if he doesn't misbehave, and, as everybody knows, the drunker he is the steadier he drives. Well, we must get along. Remember me to your mother, Jill.'

'Thanks, I will.'

Looking back, Bony saw the girl watching the car on its way back to the main track.

'Fine-looking lass,' he said when the Madden homestead had retreated into the river trees.

'Yes. The mother made a mistake.'

'Oh! A bad one?'

'The husband died a bit over two years ago. The widow hired a feller off the track. Seemed all right, just a hand looking for a job. After a year she married him. He sort of took over the place, or seemed to. Personally, I don't like him. Officially, I've nothing against him. Oily type. The booze makes him very polite, but you can see in his eyes he's not so polite in his mind.'

'The place seems a trifle run down,' Bony said. 'Many sheep?'

'About three thousand. Not a big selection when the poor country is taken out. Madden seemed to do well, though. He kept the homestead tidy and the house in good order. Now, as I said, the widow made a mistake.'

Conversation became desultory until they passed

the famous Dunlop homestead. The history of that place engaged Constable Lucas for a mile or two; then he again became quiet until Bony asked whether there was anything on his mind.

'Yes, there's something nagging, Inspector. Did you notice anything wrong with that Madden homestead?'

'Yes,' replied Bony. 'House wanted paint. The surroundings needed tidying. The shearing-shed roof is going to blow off for need of renailing.'

'I don't mean all that. Fact is, I don't know what I mean.'

'Something in the girl's demeanour?'

'No. She was normal. Never did have any time for the stepfather, and don't wonder at that. It was something wrong with the house.'

'Ah, the house! Never having seen it before, I'm afraid I cannot help you. Could it be the axe lying on the ground near the front door? The condition of the axe indicated it had been relegated to the woodheap.'

'No, it wasn't the axe. Something else. It'll come.'

The western fringe of Bourke was in sight when Constable Lucas vented a sharp exclamation.

'I have it! Funny how the mind stops and starts like a traffic signal,' he said. 'It was the old door back again. Now why?'

'The door returned home,' Bony prompted. 'So!'

'The house fronts the river, and the back is to the west and the road. It gets the westerlies and the dust. Like the rest of the place the back door became cracked for the need of putty and paint. I called there about three months ago to see Mrs Madden about a stock return, and found Lush putting on a new door;

the old one was leaning against the wall. That old door was a heavy affair with inset panels. The new one was of plain wall-board clamped to a frame. Now today the old door is back on again. Why put on an old door in place of a new one?'

'Could it not be that the plain door, more suited to the inside, was fitted to an inside door frame, and the old door rehung until a new back door could be purchased?' asked Bony.

'Yes, that's the answer. Must be the answer. Let's see, now. The axe! What would the axe be doing so far from the wood-heap?'

Bony chuckled, saying, 'You are a suspicious policeman.'

'Me, suspicious?' Lucas laughed without restraint. Then: 'It was you who brought the axe into it.'

Chapter Three

Where Is William Lush?

Circumstances rather than inherent tendencies had made Mrs Cosgrove a hard business-woman, and she could be generous. Now in her late forties, and a widow, she took a close interest in her pastoral property, Mira.

It was Thursday when the mail car made its return run from White Bend to Bourke, leaving the township at eight and collecting the mail at the Mira–Madden boxes at nine in the morning. Immediately after breakfast, taken punctually at seven, Mrs Cosgrove and her manager proceeded to complete the outward mail to be sealed into a blue bag and taken to the roadside box.

Today, her son Raymond carried the outward bag to the box, and naturally he was interested to find Lush's utility still there. He had walked this morning, following the right bank of the dry river to the sharp angle above Mira where he could see the vehicle on the cliff above the great hole filled with water.

Skirting the edge of the waterhole, he climbed the far bank and circled the abandoned machine in search of tracks that would show whether Lush had recently returned to it. The wind had played havoc with the tracks left by Lucas and Bony, and there were none more distinct.

The previous day, when he had taken the down bag from the red-headed driver, they had agreed that Lush must be suffering a hangover; today they agreed that he must have cleared out with a supply of grog and be holed up in bliss.

Raymond Cosgrove was an easy-going young man not addicted to hating people. He had, however, a strong aversion to William Lush for particularly private reasons. Where Lush was this scintillating morning didn't bother him, and he returned to the homestead unperturbed by the thought that the man might have fallen over the cliff-like bank above the waterhole and drowned. He reported the still abandoned utility to his mother.

'I know,' Mrs Cosgrove said. 'Lucas has just rung asking about that utility. He found it there yesterday on his way to Bourke and saw it again last night on his way down. He wants to know if it's still there. Ring him.'

Watching her son standing at the wall telephone, she again experienced a little pride in his lean, hard body and handsome, boyish profile – a pride which always overcame her disappointment at his refusal to take up any career but that of a sheepman.

'Sounds like the old demon,' Ray was saying. 'How's things? The ute? Yes, still there by the boxes. Signs of him? No. No, no booze or anything. Must have gone bush to tank up on his own. Be in trouble! The bastard's always in trouble.' The crude word caused Mrs Cosgrove to frown. 'All right, Sherlock. Yes, I'll do that and contact you again later.'

Turning to his mother after replacing the instrument, he said Lucas wanted them to raise Mrs Lush and check on her husband.

'I'll speak to her, Ray.'

To save Madden expense, Mrs Cosgrove's husband had consented to the telephone line being brought over the river direct to his office, where the switchboard was installed to permit outlet to the White Bend exchange. Now the son made the connection, and Mrs Cosgrove heard Jill Madden's voice.

'Hullo, Jill. Is your stepfather home? Ray has just come from the box and found his utility still abandoned.'

'We haven't seen him since he left for town,' Jill said, betraying slight agitation. 'Yesterday Mr Lucas called about seeing the ute. It seems that Lush went off to drink alone and is still at it. He'll come home when he's ready. I'd have gone for the ute, but mother's ill. She wasn't well yesterday and got up and fell, and she's hurt herself.'

'How badly, Jill?' Mrs Cosgrove asked sharply.

'Well, she hurt her face when she fell on a low stool, and her ribs are hurt, too. I've done what I can, Mrs Cosgrove; liniment and bandages – all that. She's sleeping just now.'

'Now that *is* bad,' agreed the elder woman. 'You must ring if your mother isn't rested after sleeping. I'll leave the line open. Meanwhile I'll send all the hands out to locate your stepfather – that is, the men available.' Hanging up, she spoke to her son. 'Lush isn't home, and Mrs Lush has had a fall and hurt herself badly. Take the men on hand and look for the drunken sot. You go too, Mac. Do you good to get on a horse. You're putting on too much weight.'

Where Is William Lush?

Ian MacCurdle, sandy of hair and moustache, tall and rugged, inwardly groaned and followed young Cosgrove from the office. He had come to Mira when Cosgrove was alive, and now was like a piece of the furniture.

Mrs Cosgrove heard her son shouting men's names, and from the narrow veranda of the office-store building she watched him and four others riding down-river to the easier crossing below the shearing-shed; she knew their objective was to beat through Madman's Bend, a huge wasteland of billabongs and arid flats, and so out to the mail-box and the utility.

They had not returned when the house cook gonged for lunch, and before leaving Mrs Cosgrove rang through to Madden's Selection.

'Mother is still asleep, Mrs Cosgrove,' was Jill's report. 'I'm getting worried. I think . . . I don't know what to think.'

Never hesitant in making a decision, Mrs Cosgrove said she would leave immediately and, calling for the housemaid, told her to delay lunch and then station herself at the office telephone till she returned or Mr Mac came back. Following the faint path along the river bank, made by her son and others who had gone for the mail, she could hear men shouting on the far side in Madman's Bend, and eventually saw two of them at the utility. She crossed the dry bed of the river opposite the Madden house and so came to the front door. Jill Madden let her in.

'Oh, thank you for coming, Mrs Cosgrove,' Jill said. 'Mother seems to be worse.'

Bill Lush's victim was unconscious. Her face, from which some of the bandages had been removed,

19

shocked Mrs Cosgrove, and, having examined the woman's right side and abdomen, she blamed herself for not having come much earlier.

'I'll call the doctor,' she said crisply, fearing the girl would lose self-control. 'It would be silly to take your mother to Bourke. I'll get through to Superintendent Macey. He'll fix the doctor.'

She had to direct her maid in her office to work the board, and then had to wait while someone in the Superintendent's office went and found him. She felt relief when she heard his deep voice.

'We're in trouble, Jim,' she said. 'My neighbour, Mrs Lush, has had a very bad fall and needs the doctor. She's unconscious, and her breathing is irregular. Now you know what Dr Leveska is, but he must come down as quickly as possible. Will you get him into the air at once?'

'Yes, of course, Betsy. That is, if he isn't away. Just a minute.'

She heard another voice say, 'I could hear the name Lush. Ask if Lush is still absent.' Then: 'All right. Betsy, we'll get the doctor on his way. Is Lush not there?'

'My men are out searching for him.' Her voice was raised when she added, 'You should have him put on the Blackfellers' Act.'

'We might try at that, after what I've heard from Constable Lucas. Can I tell the doctor you'll have the wind indicator out on your strip? Save time, you know.'

Mrs Cosgrove said she would have it done, and then asked Jill for a cup of tea and whatever there was in the larder. Alone with the unconscious woman. she did what she thought prudent for her, thinking that it must have been an involved accident to have brought Jill's mother to this.

'When did it happen?' she asked Jill later at lunch.

'The night before last, Mrs Cosgrove.' The girl's dark eyes met steadily the grey eyes of her guest. 'In spite of what mother has said so often about not saying anything because of scandal, I'll have to let it out now. She mightn't recover. She might die, mightn't she?'

'It's a chance. How did it happen?'

Jill told of what she had found on her return after Lush's departure for town, and what her mother had told her about the assault. Mrs Cosgrove listened with growing anger. She wanted to upbraid the girl, but refrained, knowing how independent bush folk are, and how reluctant they are to admit scandal affecting them. The two women were still seated at the table when the telephone rang.

'They've just left,' said the Superintendent. 'That is, Doc Leveska and Inspector Bonaparte. The Inspector would like to have a look around, perhaps do a little fishing and shooting. You won't mind?'

'I'll let you know later if it's a pleasure or not. When are you and your wife visiting us? I'm finding the need to gossip.'

'Not before the flood. We could be caught there a long time. Did you have the wind indicator put in place?'

'Heavens, no! I forgot about it. I'll see to it at once.' To the girl she said, 'The doctor has left, and I promised to put out the indicator.' Manipulating the instrument she contacted the maid. 'The men home yet, Ethel?'

'Not ye. Mrs Cosgrove. Steve was here a moment ago wanting to know if he had to keep their lunch.'

'Of course he has to. Run along and tell him to come to the phone.'

Mrs Cosgrove waited impatiently to hear the groom's voice. She told him to take the wind indicator out to the strip, to use the grey truck, and to wait there for Doctor Leveska. She was annoyed with herself, for it was only ninety-eight miles from Bourke, and the doctor might arrive before the indicator was in place.

He was a good physician, but often offensive. Although he was a good airman, he often refused to fly when in one of his moods, which people thought were associated with a bottle. This was why Mrs Cosgrove sought his aid through her friend, the Superintendent in Charge of the Western Division.

Seated again at the table, she regarded Jill Madden. The girl was rolling a cigarette, and after she had lit it she said, 'If Mother dies, will they hang Lush?'

'No, they molly-coddle murderers in this state. But they'll put him away for a few years. You should find that a relief. Did he ever strike her before this last time?'

Jill nodded.

'If Mother doesn't die, if she gets well again, what will they do to Lush?'

'I believe nothing, unless your mother complains to the police.'

'She'll never do that. If he does attack her again I shall shoot him.'

Mrs Cosgrove slowly shook her head, saying, 'It would make bad worse. It would be justifiable homicide if you shot him while he was actually attacking your mother, or about to attack you, but I was thinking of the after-effects: court hearings, publicity, and the rest. Your mother must be persuaded to complain to the police, and he might be sent to jail for six months. Might, because it's more likely he would be put on a bond of good behaviour.'

Mrs Cosgrove was to recall this conversation, and she pondered on the wretched lives of these two women while, despite the girl's protests, she helped with the washing of the lunch utensils and the general tidying. She was again looking down at the unconscious woman when a car was heard approaching.

It was Constable Lucas. His hazel eyes were stern, but he was gentle with Jill and, after looking at the woman on the bed, announced that he had been ordered to come by his Superintendent.

'Lush still absent, I suppose?'

'Yes, Mr Lucas, still absent,' Mrs Cosgrove told him. 'You may have to track him for murder. My son and the men are searching for him, as we told you.'

'Jill, has this sort of thing happened before?'

The girl admitted that it had.

'Then why the devil didn't you say what happened this time when I was here yesterday? What stopped you?'

'Mother. She always dreaded scandal. And she wasn't like she is when you called yesterday.'

They were in the living-room-kitchen, off which were three rooms. Lucas casually looked about and noted the three doors. They were all of the heavy, old-fashioned type. He found the axe outside where he had previously seen it, and was about to stroll around when he heard voices from the river and went to tell the women the doctor was here.

Doctor Leveska was slight, sharp of feature, bright of eye, and acidulous of tongue when he said, 'What's been going on here? How did she fall? Couldn't be hurt that bad she couldn't have been brought up to the hospital. Now, where is she?'

Jill and Mrs Cosgrove went with him into the bedroom. Lucas and Bonaparte remained in the living-room. In the bedroom it was very quiet until Jill Madden broke into sobs, and Doctor Leveska came out. He said softly, 'She just died, Lucas. And it was no fall.'

Chapter Four

Bony Takes Command

After receiving Constable Lucas's report by telephone and being told that Doctor Leveska insisted on an autopsy, Superintendent Macey instructed Lucas to obtain statements from Jill Madden and Mrs Cosgrove and convey the body to Bourke. Action was prompted by the flood now rolling past Bourke; it would certainly cut off both Madden's Selection and Mira, perhaps for weeks.

Mrs Cosgrove insisted on taking Jill to her own homestead. When the two women and Doctor Leveska had gone, Bony helped Lucas to service Lush's utility for the trip to Bourke, and together they placed the body on the vehicle.

'I'll remain until you return,' Bony told Lucas. 'I'll look around meanwhile. If Lush turns up I'll hold him.'

'I can't see that plain door hung to an inside frame,' Lucas said, and Bony said he would look for it.

After the constable had gone he wandered through the house and made sure the door was neither in use nor stored. Then he rekindled the stove fire and brewed a pot of tea, which he sipped while sitting at the table. He was beginning to think there could be a perfectly simple solution to the mystery of the missing door.

The door and the axe on the ground outside the back entrance, plus the continued absence of Lush, had decided him to cut his scheduled departure from Bourke. He was like a beagle testing the air, and like the beagle he had to follow the scent to its source. He had spent the morning in Macey's office writing his report on the investigation of a crime far out from White Bend. The results of the investigation had pleased the Superintendent, who because of an outbreak of influenza, was short-staffed and raised no serious objection to Bony's cancelling the afternoon air trip to Sydney. Mrs Macey was serving their lunch when the clerk came to say that Mrs Cosgrove was ringing from Madden's Selection. Bony had accompanied the Superintendent to the office, there to learn that Lush had not returned home.

'Very well, Bonaparte,' Macey had said. 'If Leveska will take you it would help. But you'll be doing your own washing if the Commissioner bursts the collar off his neck.'

'I find commissioners easier to deal with than constables,' Bony had said blandly. 'That girl said nothing to Lucas about her mother having fallen and so injured herself that this morning she is in a coma and Mrs Cosgrove is much alarmed. The change of doors could have a simple answer, but you'll agree that changing a good one for an old one isn't normal procedure.'

The girl was so upset that it had been difficult to obtain a statement from her covering the assault by her stepfather, and neither Lucas nor Bony had bothered her about the doors. Now, sitting at the table, Bony found himself in a commanding position to undertake a new investigation which might or might not become interesting enough to hold him to Madden's Selection.

Having smoked one of his badly-made cigarettes, he examined the rear door. The hinges were as old as the door, and the insets into the frame were longer by an inch, proving that a succession of doors had been hinged to it. He swung the present door. It squeaked. The paint was blistered by sun and wind. Dust clung heavily to the panel surrounds, as thick on the inside as the outside. There was no dust on the inside window-sills, no dust on the dresser shelves or the mantel, and no dust on the top of the skirting-boards, proving that Mrs Madden and her daughter were meticulous housekeepers and that the old and dusty door had recently been rehung.

He recalled seeing a Winchester repeating rifle leaning in a corner at one end of the dresser, and he drew it forward with one fingertip to the muzzle of the barrel. The barrel gleamed with oil, as did the stock. Fingerprints! Likely, but not important at the moment. Nor, at the moment, was there anything odd about it having been cleaned.

There was, however, possible significance in the circular hole in the ceiling. Bony brought a step-ladder from the outside wash-house. He estimated the size of the hole as being close to the size of a ·32 bullet. He moved the ladder and, mounting it again, lifted the manhole, covering himself with sand and dust. Above the hole in the ceiling he could see a corresponding hole in the iron roof. The rifle he had cursorily examined was a ·32.

He was putting the ladder away in the wash-house

when he saw a horseman coming from the mail-boxes, and he sat on the outside bench and waited, his fingers busy with the usual cigarette. Presently the rider dismounted and, with the reins looped in an arm, came to the bench. He was young and fair.

'Who are you?' he asked.

'I am Inspector Bonaparte.'

'Oh! How's the old lady?'

'Dead. Who are you?'

'I'm Cosgrove. Did you say dead?'

'Yes. Didn't you know?'

'No. I've been out all morning with the men, trying to locate Lush. I knew on leaving that Mrs Madden had hurt herself in a fall. What goes? Isn't Jill about?'

Bony said that Jill had gone with Mrs Cosgrove, who had invited her to stay at Mira. When young Cosgrove remarked on the presence of Lucas's jeep and was told the reason for it he fastened the horse's reins to a veranda post and sat on the bench.

'What are you an inspector of—rabbits?'

'No. Police.'

'Crikey! Then you'll be wanting to put the old hand on Lush?'

'Of course.'

'Add the boot to the hand, good and hard.' Ray Cosgrove was rolling a cigarette with hands between his parted knees, and the rim of his stetson appeared to be aimed at the ground. 'You know, to call Lush a swine is to insult the pigs. He's a polite, mealy-mouthed, unadulterated, vicious bastard. What the old girl and Jill put up with nobody knows. I hope it's me who finds him, because if it's you he'll end up in a nice comfortable jail for a year or two.'

28

'Should it be you who finds him?'

'That's a little secret, Inspector.' Cosgrove sat up and leaned back against the house wall.

'You have a personal interest?'

'Naturally, the Maddens being our neighbours since the year one. Jill's father was a sound feller. He and my dad were friends. When he died this place was flourishing. Now look at it: litter and rubbish all over, the sheds coming adrift, the fences propped up instead of repaired. Why did Lush hit his wife this time, d'you know?'

'She refused to give him a cheque for three hundred pounds.'

'Three hundred!' said Cosgrove. 'Quite a wad. Must have been in deep at White Bend. There's a poker school down there. Run by two brothers named Roberts. You don't pay up, you get it rough. They must have given Lush a lot of rope.'

'He drinks, doesn't he?' said Bony.

'Too right, but not more than most of us when we go to town. And I did hear that the hotel stopped his credit. Besides, again like most of us, he would have brought a carton or two of beer back with him, but when I took the mail to the box day before yesterday, which was the morning after the night he left town, there wasn't a bottle in his ute, let alone a reasonably good supply.'

'Then you believe he must have been desperately in need of three hundred pounds to settle a gambling debt?'

'He'd have been just as desperate if he wanted only fifty,' answered Cosgrove. 'The Roberts have a reputation, as I said. Mind you, if that slit-eyed skunk was refused five bob he'd have bashed his wife just the same. According to Jill it had got to be a pleasant hobby with him.'

'Have you a theory of what happened when he left his utility?' Bony asked, and Cosgrove slowly shook his head.

'Not much of an idea, but, knowing the swine, when he didn't come home he could have walked over the cliff into the hole and drowned, or he could have holed up somewhere about here with a case of something to keep him company. Have you been through the place?'

'Not as yet,' replied Bony.

'I decided to do so. It's why I came. Shall we give it a go now?'

Bony agreed, and, having put the horse in the yard, they began a tour of inspection. In the open-fronted motor-shed was a worn sulky, the gear hanging on a wall peg. Cosgrove said that Lush went in for a trotter but had never won a race with it, dropping more money down the drain. They entered a two-man hut furnished with only a table and two iron bedsteads. The door sagged, and the window was massed with cobweb. The compact shearing-shed offered no clue, and after leaving it they parted, young Cosgrove circling away from the river, and Bony keeping to the bank on the return to the house. There was a natural hole below the shed, and water was raised from it by a pump to tanks serving both the shed and the house.

Eventually Bony came to a small yard and gallows where ration sheep were yarded and killed. Draped over a rail were several sheepskins long since dry enough to be removed into the skin-shed. Bony looked into the shed and found no evidence of its having been occupied. A short distance from the gallows was a fireplace roughly constructed with large stones in a semicircle to provide a windbreak. Here rubbish such as dog bones and kitchen refuse had been burnt, and from here to the house ran a distinct path.

The condition of the top layer of ash showed that the latest burning had been quite recent, and the spread of it indicated that much material had been consumed. The two door hinges, blackened by heat, were spaced as they had been when screwed to a door; the door lock and handles were there too.

Bony looked for Cosgrove, saw him nearing the house, and proceeded along the path to join him.

'I couldn't cut his tracks,' Cosgrove said. 'Well, you can see what a loafing bastard he was. Did nothing about the place. Bad enough to make poor old Madden turn over six times in a run. What's your plans? What about the dogs and the chooks?'

'It was finally arranged that I should stay here to welcome Mr Lush, and inhabit the place until such time as something else is decided,' Bony replied. 'There's chook feed in the motor-shed and a quarter of mutton in the meat-house. I could see only two dogs, so we should not perish of starvation. Mrs Cosgrove is having my case sent from your homestead.'

Cosgrove smiled for the first time since he had appeared.

'All right, Inspector. Let the chap know if you want anything when he brings your duds. You'll know Lush when you see him. Has a face like a crumpet. I'll keep in touch, too, about the river. I can hear old Leveska getting off the ground.' Freeing the reins from the post, he flicked the off-side one over the horse's head, bunched them, and then appeared to be lifted by jet air-stream into the saddle. His final words were: 'Bet you find the radio in order. Lush would be sure to have that right to listen to the race results.'

He rode away to cross the river bed above the shearing-shed. Bony unchained the two dogs, which began to race about and pretend to chase the fowls. The roosters screeched, and the excitement brought several kookaburras to perch on a roughly made stand and there set up a chorus of laughter. The place had come alive, and Bony took possession.

With the woodheap axe he chopped and split enough wood to keep the stove going. Then he filled the oil lamps, and inspected Mrs Lush's linen cupboard. He made up a bed in the third bedroom, brewed a pot of tea, and took a spell with several cigarettes. Once more energetic, he cut up the forequarter of mutton, providing a shoulder for roasting, chops for grilling, and a meal for the dogs.

The kookaburras watched him conveying meat to the house, their wonderful eyes beady and seemingly expectant. As he entered the living-room one muttered and another began a cackling laugh. He returned to look more closely at the perch-stand, and then, seeing stains along the wood, knew what it was for and why the birds made no attempt to fly at his approach. They, too, demanded dinner, and there were eight of them.

The fowl-house was inside a high-netted yard to protect the birds from foxes. When Bony appeared again with a dish of wheat and proceeded to the yard, clucking for the birds to follow, they ignored him. Hang it, the fellow was a stranger! Inside the yard he clucked louder than ever, and now the two dogs went into action. They mustered the fowls in through the gateway as they would muster sheep into a yard.

Bony had rewarded the dogs with their meal and decided not to chain them for the night when his attention was again drawn to the waiting kookaburras by soft hooting and low, broken chuckling. Happily he cut meat into small pieces and took it to the platform-perch affair. The kookaburras barely bothered to make room for the meat to be put on it, and they evinced no ill manners by gobbling or squabbling.

'One can learn much of people from their animals and birds,' he told them. 'The girl would have tamed you, my wild friends. The man probably trained the dogs, and the wife doubtless raised the fowls and dusted the house every day of her life – save for the inside of the old back door.'

Bony was at dinner when a man suddenly appeared in the frame supporting the old door. He was not William Lush because his face was long and unlike a crumpet. The two dogs, now wagging tails of welcome, had not barked a warning of his coming. Bony invited him in, and he entered carrying the suitcase and a letter.

'Brought your case, Inspector,' he said. 'A letter from Mrs Cosgrove, too. Said for me to wait for any answer.'

'Thanks. Have a cup of tea?'

'Just had dinner.'

Bony read: 'Jill Madden says you are to make free of the house. Bed linen and blankets in the linen cupboard and meat in the meat-house. Please give the dogs a bone, and lock up the chooks, and please feed the kookaburras. They will be waiting on the dinner perch. My son will call early in the morning.' It was signed 'Betsy Cosgrove.'

Bony looked up at the waiting man.

33

'There ⸱ no answer. What's your name?'

'Vickory. Vic Vickory. I'm the Mira overseer.'

'Tell me, Mr Vickory, why did Mrs Cosgrove trouble to write this note when there is the telephone?'

'Oh! She said she couldn't raise you, and thought you must be out looking for Lush.'

Bony rose and manipulated the wall telephone. There was no connection.

Shrugging, he said, 'The line is broken somewhere. Now there is a message for Mrs Cosgrove. Ask her, please, to have the line repaired first thing in the morning.'

'I will, Inspector. Good night.'

Chapter Five

One Frosty Night and Morning

Bony sat on the bench outside the back door and watched the sun go down in a clear, dustless sky, its rays coldly lemon. The kelpie dog lay under the bench beneath him, and the other, a border collie, lay on the ground a yard or so from him. The kookaburras departed to perch in the same gum tree and join in an evening chorus of gargantuan mirth on the high notes and sinister cackling on the low. And, when the fowls had ceased their quarrelling about who should roost with whom, the peaceful silence of the evening was itself a kind of lullaby.

It was quite dark when Bony heard a car coming down the river track. He wondered who it could be. He could not expect Constable Lucas, and traffic hereabouts was remarkable for its scarcity: not a vehicle had passed since the policeman had left. The dogs sat and listened, and the kelpie growled. Then to the right appeared a white glow, which grew like a searchlight and continued along the road, passing the house almost a mile to the west

When the second car announced its coming to the dogs it was after nine o'clock. It turned off at the junction and aimed its headlights at the house. Both dogs stood, the smaller leaning stiffly against Bony's leg. Bony patted him and ordered them to be quiet. The car stopped, the headlights were switched off, and Constable Lucas said, cheerfully, 'I hope the kettle's boiling. Why the blackout?'

'We were communing with the stars,' replied Bony, and led the way inside to light the lamps and then add fuel to the stove. The dogs stayed outside, as is customary at homesteads.

'Hard trip?' Bony asked.

'Fairish,' replied Lucas. 'Had a blow-out that kept me, and the Super demanded details of this and that. How did you do?'

'Loafed, made pals with the dogs, was visited by the Mira overseer who brought my case, and fed the stock, which includes eight kookaburras. I have half a dozen nice chops I'll grill for you. You'll stay?'

'For the chops, yes. Then it's on my way. I mentioned the door changes to the Super, and he seemed impressed. Did you come across the new one?'

'What did the Super say about them?' Bony asked. The table was covered by a cloth, and, having made tea, he laid a place for the constable. Lucas grinned, but his eyes remained serious.

'Said you are a known bloody bloodhound, Inspector. Said you could scent crime before it was committed, and that when you didn't return with the doctor you had certainly sniffed it. And then what? Orders me to go back to my station and to accept any instructions you give. Oh, there's something else. I am to tell you that he telegraphed for permission to hand the job to you, said permission being received at six-thirty p.m.'

'Kind of him, but unnecessary. I gave myself permission.' Bony smiled, and his brilliant blue eyes beamed. Looking away from their magnetism, Lucas once again noted the dark face, the Nordic features, and for a moment fell beneath the spell this man of two races could exert. The aroma of grilling lamb chops sharpened his hunger, and over the teacup he asked again about the missing door. The slight incongruity of an inspector grilling chops for a constable, first-class, did not occur to him, but then the inspector was not in full uniform.

'The new door was burnt yesterday,' Bony said, and withdrew a wood sliver from the stove to light a cigarette.

'Ah! It was, eh? Where?'

'The site doesn't matter. The fact is interesting. The old one was rehung after Mrs Lush was knocked about.'

'Then something happened to the new one.'

'Something happened to it, something which could not be repaired and the door repainted.'

'Funny. You make anything of it?' asked the policeman.

'Not much. The women could have locked Lush out before he went to town, or after he came back on foot from the mail-boxes. I can see him, angry at being refused money, going to the shed for his utility, bringing it back to the house and making another effort to extract a cheque from his wife. When he found the door locked against him he went to the woodheap for the old axe and smashed it in. And, such was his fury, attacked his wife.'

'It could have been that way. Being locked out boiled him over.'

'Then Mrs Lush persuaded the girl on her return

37

home to remove the damaged door and destroy it to prevent talk should anyone call.'

Lucas agreed that that accounted for the change, but he might not have done so had he been told about the hole in the ceiling now in the shadow cast by the lampshade.

'What do you know about two men named Roberts?' asked Bony.

'The town butchers. They live a mile out of town on a small holding property. I've never had trouble from them, although I've suspected they gamble. At home, of course. Cards, not two-up. As they own the property I can do nothing when they invite friends there for a game. Why? They interest you?'

'The girl said, remember, that Lush wanted three hundred pounds, that he was desperate for the money. Young Cosgrove told me that Lush's credit at the hotel was restricted. He told me also that the Roberts men played it rough when a gambling debt was owed them. I am interested to learn why Lush needed all that money. You might make discreet inquiries. Is there a lawyer at White Bend?'

Lucas said there was not. Asked whether he happened to know who looked after Mrs Lush's affairs, he said he didn't know. While he ate, Bony questioned him about the Cosgroves and their men, and afterwards asked him to describe how Lush walked, going so far as to request a demonstration.

'I'll have to try to pick up his tracks, which will be difficult, not having seen them,' he went on. 'I am beginning to think that the theory of Lush going bush with a store of booze is no longer well founded. He was short of money, and his credit at the hotel was short, too. You might go into this credit angle. Again, he wasn't in town long enough to indulge in a long bender and so leave on the verge of delirium tremens. I'll tell you something to add spice to your inquiries. In the ceiling above us is a bullet hole, and in the corner there is the rifle from which the bullet was probably fired.'

The policeman's fair eyebrows shot upward, and the operation of loading his pipe was halted.

'The hole in the ceiling was made recently, Lucas. The ceiling is of plaster and is stained with smoke, but the edges of the hole are plaster-white. Above it is a corresponding hole in the iron roof. Further, the rifle has been cleaned and oiled. And I haven't found another of the same calibre. There's a shotgun and a Winchester single-shot forty-four, and neither has received such care. Better take them with you. They may be needed.'

Lucas continued filling his pipe, and said nothing until he had applied a match and was smoking. Then he said, 'It draws pictures, doesn't it?'

'Dimly. However, it does shadow the girl's story with doubt. As I may not be able to telephone the Super without being heard by someone at Mira, I'd like you to tell him that I am finding this business of great interest. Just that: no details. D'you know if young Cosgrove is in love with Jill Madden?'

'No, I don't, Inspector. We haven't been long enough at White Bend to hear much gossip.'

'We! Who is included? Your wife?'

'She knows everyone, and, as blotting-paper absorbs water, she absorbs the affairs of other people without giving up anything about us. Been useful more than once. I'll get her to find out that one.'

39

'Do. Now for this flood. When d'you think it will reach this point?'

'It could be in a couple of days,' replied Lucas. 'I'm told that following the head the body of water flows fast. I've never seen a real flood along this river, but they say it has widened out from its banks for twenty miles, and they told me only this evening that what's coming is an old-man flood. You'll have to watch it.'

'I shall retreat to Mira, or get away to White Bend ahead of it in the utility.'

'You could take the track out to the back of this property. There's a well and hut bordering the outside road to Bourke and down to the Bend. But don't delay after the flood head passes, because between here and that outside road there's two creeks that will flood back quick and cut you off. This house will beat the flood rise, but I don't suppose it has enough grub to keep you going for a month.'

'Well, you should be going now. If there is anything else I'll contact you somehow.'

Having watched Lucas depart in his jeep, Bony called the dogs inside, and was amused when neither would obey. Being a little mystified by the broken line to Mira, he needed the dogs to give warning of anything that might eventuate, even the return of Lush; so he pulled them by their collars into the living-room and closed and locked the door.

Having been fussed over, they quickly forgot the taboo, and followed him about the house while he tested the front door and the windows. He drew an old rocking-chair to the stove and settled there to meditate and plan his future activities.

It was daybreak when he woke coldly stiff. He opened the door and the dogs ran out. Going to the woodheap for chips with which to fire the stove he saw two milking cows standing beside the milking-shed. Frost whitened the upper surfaces of the wood-pile.

After two cups of tea and three cigarettes he milked the cows, took a cold shower of three seconds, and then cooked breakfast, at which he did not linger. He brought the step-ladder. He had found cartridges for the thirty-two, and with one of them he proved that the bullet fitted the hole in the ceiling. When he had returned the ladder and cleaned up, the old American clock registered the time as seven-twenty.

By half past seven he had run the utility into the shed and pocketed the ignition key; now he was re-lieved of responsibility for it as well as for the dogs. He had found a pair of Lush's boots, and with these he made impressions on soft ground. In size they were a small seven. The impressions gave him very little; they only proved what the sole of each indicated – that Lush walked with the toes angled slightly in-ward, as many men do who have earned a living for long years in the saddle. Without the man in them the boots gave no significant leads to character.

After locking the house Bony walked between the twin wheel-marks of vehicles leading to the road and the mail-boxes. The sun, just risen, failed to penetrate the avenue of river gums, and this side was cold and still darkly green. The kookaburras continued to greet the new day with their mocking, and Bony wondered if they would call for dinner. A magpie, gleaming black and white, whirred after a slower-flying crow that cawed with annoyance, and a flock of red and grey galah parrots rose above the avenue to speak a language all their own.

41

All seemed right with this world. All was right with Inspector Bonaparte. How William Lush was faring was a subject for speculation.

If Lush had walked from his useless utility to the house that night he would have followed this track and not the river bank, which in several places was broken by water gutters deep enough to injure a man who fell into one. Lush would have kept on or close to his own motor track. Quite soon Bony realized that the ground so far did not favour a tracker, being composed of hard clay rubble extending to the junction with the main track. From this point, however, the surface, although harder, could be broken to whitest dust by motor wheels and the hooves of a horse.

There was no difficulty in finding the exact place in which the utility had been abandoned; dust-covered oil marks gave it. Extending outwards for several yards, and about the mail-boxes some ten feet from the edge of the cliff above the waterhole, the ground registered numerous prints of men and horses, now blurred and useless.

Recalling that during the night when Lush abandoned the utility the wind had been almost at gale force, and that the following day it had blown almost half a gale, Bony stood by one of the boxes and smoked a cigarette while he took in this scene which had not been imprinted on his mind when he saw it from Lucas's jeep.

The river, after passing Madden's homestead, came south-westward to this sharp major bend at which it was turned due east. One mile farther down could be seen the reservoir tanks and the roofs of the Mira homestead atop a similar cliff-like bank above a similar water-gouged, water-filled hole. In either direction the massive red-gums formed an avenue above the empty river course. Here only, and at Mira bend, was the avenue broken, permitting the easterly wind full freedom for a mile to attack the mail-boxes, and the westerly wind the same distance to strike at the Mira homestead.

Chapter Six

Part Two of Jill's Story

Bony had to leave the angle to reach the normal bank of the river, and there he descended the steep, grey slope to the bed. The red-gums seemed to tower above him. The bed was littered by windfalls of twigs and small branches, leaves, and long streamers of shredded bark.

At the outer edge of the great hole he paused to glance upward to the cliff top, sixty to seventy feet above, and could just see the top of one of the mailboxes. It was clear that anyone falling over the cliff near those boxes would plunge into water, and should the fall take place a few yards to left or right he would crash on a narrow rock ledge between the water and the cliff base.

There was nothing to hand for testing the depth of the hole. It appeared to be very deep, for the water was clear and the bottom could not be seen. Doubtless it would contain much water-logged tree debris of trunk and branch, and had Lush fallen into it his body might well be trapped, never to rise.

A man shouted from the east bank and Bony saw young Cosgrove standing beside a horse. As Bony joined him the fair-haired man grinned his good morning and said that Jill Madden was at the house and did Bony have the keys?

'I thought it wise to lock up,' Bony said.

'I'm taking her to Bourke for the funeral, and she wants clothes and things,' Cosgrove said. 'And the telephone's all right now. A tree branch fell on the line.'

They proceeded along the east bank, Cosgrove leading his mount.

'Is the search for Lush continuing today?' asked Bony.

'Yes. The men will be going through Madman's Bend again, and then mustering the up-river bend. I don't think Lush is holed up anywhere, except down in that hole you were looking at. Still, we have to give it a go.'

'I've been trying to cut his tracks and have failed,' Bony admitted. 'Any information from Bourke this morning?'

'Superintendent Macey telephoned saying the autopsy on Mrs Madden would be done today, and that she could be buried this afternoon. Funeral timed for five o'clock.'

'Who else will be going?'

'Mother's going with us. We'll be back late because we'll have to make two wide detours. The flood's already filling billabongs and creeks for twenty miles south of Bourke. Should be here tomorrow night or the next morning. There's a hell of a lot of water above Bourke. I wouldn't delay leaving Madden's place after tomorrow evening. You could be cut off for weeks. Jill wants to pack things to take to Mira. She'll have to live there.'

Cosgrove tethered his horse opposite the small

homestead and they crossed to it. They found Jill Madden sitting on the bench outside the back door. Her dark eyes widened when Bony bowed slightly and offered condolences.

She said, 'I can't take it all in, Inspector. Mother and I were very close. Mrs Cosgrove's been very kind, and I must thank you for looking after the place. You even milked the cows, I see.'

'Yes, I attended to everything bar the cats.' Bony regarded the two on the bench. 'They must have cleared out, being frightened of strangers. What's going to happen to everything?'

'Mrs Cosgrove is having the cows and fowls and dogs and cats all moved over the river, and what I'll pack up for myself. Can I ask you something?'

She was standing, the keys in hand, infinitely more feminine than when Bony had first seen her. He thought she would be still more so if she arranged her hair differently. It gleamed blackly and promised to look luxuriant if permitted.

She said, 'Have you found any sign of my step-father?'

'As I've told Mr Cosgrove, I have been trying to cut his tracks. It is hardly time for questions, but there are several I'll have to ask you, Inside, perhaps?'

'Yes, of course. I'm sorry.'

'You start your packing and we'll fire the stove and brew tea. Tell us what to do to help,' Bony said. 'We can talk later.'

'All right. And you have actually washed up everything and tidied.'

'I have been thoroughly domesticated, Miss Madden,' Bony boasted as he lit paper beneath the chips he had pushed into the range.

46

The small bedroom was open, and the girl said, 'And you've even made your bed.'

'More than I've ever done,' Cosgrove boasted, cheerfully trying to lighten the gloom. 'Sing out if you want a hand, Jill.'

The girl went to her room and proceeded to pack clothes into a suitcase. Like every woman, she had, of course, nothing to wear, but Bony noticed her filling a second large case, and then she was asking Cosgrove to fetch two wood cases from the laundry. Assisted by Cosgrove, she packed into these the office books and records, and several books, among which was a large family Bible. At last she was done, and Bony poured tea into the cups he had placed on the table together with a cake he had found in a tin.

'Think you have all you'll want?' asked Cosgrove. 'What about the kitchen sink?'

'I think we'll leave it, Ray,' she said, essaying a wan smile. 'The small case I'll take over now to go to Bourke with. What will you be doing, Inspector?'

'With your permission I'd like to stay until to-morrow. Your stepfather could turn up, you know.'

'And you'd arrest him for what he did to Mother?'

'I would do that.'

'Stay as long as you like, or as long as the flood will let you.' Her mouth became grim, probably from long practice, and her eyes became hard, giving her face a hint of wild anger.

'He's a simpering, foul beast,' she said softly. 'I hope he will resist arrest and that you'll have to shoot him.' Involuntarily she glanced at the corner where the oiled rifle had been, and from it looked directly at Bony. 'Someone's taken his gun.'

'I removed it with the others, Miss Madden,' he

said, and she saw his eyes widen and felt herself irresistibly held by them. 'I thought you would not want another shot fired through the ceiling.'

Cosgrove looked upward, and so did the girl, pretending astonishment and failing to deceive. The young man said nothing, and the girl fell to staring beyond the open panel door. Bony said, 'The old door is of interest, Miss Madden, because recently it was put on there in place of a new one. The new one was burnt to ash at the killing-yard. Can you tell me why?'

Jill Madden continued to stare through the doorway at the sun-lit country. Cosgrove pursed his lips, looking from her to Bony and back to her.

'Yes, I'll tell you,' she said, again softly. 'It doesn't matter now, not now that Mother's dead and can't any more be afraid of gossip and shame and hurt. That night I sat up with the rifle and waited for Lush to come home. When he did he found the doors and windows locked. When I wouldn't let him in he went for the woodheap axe and began smashing the door in. I fired a shot into the ceiling to warn him. When I saw the axe coming in through the door I fired at it to give him a fright.'

Her voice ceased, and Bony added, 'And killed him.'

'No. I sat with my back to the wall there all night. After I fired through the door there wasn't a sound. I thought I might have killed him, I thought he might be foxing and would try to break in through one of the windows, and I had my mind made up that if he did I'd shoot him dead.

'It was a terrible night, just listening for him, expecting to hear him breaking in at any moment, and Mother in her room moaning with the pain he'd given her. Towards morning I felt sure he was lying dead outside the door, and when it was light and I opened it he wasn't there.

'I didn't know what to do then. Mother called, and I went to her, and she wanted to know if she'd heard a shot in the night, and I told her what had happened. I wasn't sure she understood till she said to take the door off and put on the old one in case anyone called and saw it and would guess what had happened. I got her to take a little tea, and gave her aspirin tablets, and then I went looking for Lush.

'I took the rifle with me. I went to the men's hut, and then into the sheds. I couldn't see him, although I kept shouting for him. When I came in again Mother was asleep, or I thought then she was, and so I took the damaged door off and put on the old one, and then burnt the damaged one, as you found out. That's all, except that I sat a while and then couldn't rouse Mother, and rang Mrs Cosgrove.'

While the girl was speaking Bony rolled a cigarette; noticing her looking at it he offered it to her, and almost blindly she took it.

'Why didn't you admit all that to Constable Lucas when he took down your statement?'

'Same thing, Inspector. Prevent scandal,' interposed Cosgrove.

'Please,' Bony admonished him.

'It was as Ray says,' Jill Madden agreed. 'Lush wasn't outside anywhere. He must have run away, perhaps for good and all. So why say anything about it?'

'You may yet regret having kept silent, Miss Madden. For the time being, however, neither of you

49

will mention it to anyone. Should Lush turn up, it
will not be important.'

'If he doesn't turn up, it will be, eh?' asked
Cosgrove.

'Certain deductions will follow such an eventuality,
for if he isn't found alive or dead there can be no
proof that he walked or ran from the door alive. That
is why I chose to ask you both not to speak of it to
anyone.'

'But can't you believe what Jill says?'

'I fear not, although I permit myself to hope she
speaks the truth. I shall continue to add my efforts
to those of the Mira men to find Lush. Now, don't
you think you had better leave for Mira and Bourke?
Don't worry about your things, Miss Madden, or
about the animals. You may be assured of my sympathy. I'd like to ask you two a question you might
think impertinent. May I?'

Jill Madden looked at Cosgrove, and he nodded.

'Are you two in love?'

To this both nodded, and the girl began to sob.
Cosgrove took her hand, saying, 'We found out about
it a couple of months ago, Inspector. We had to keep
it dark because my mother detests Lush, and anyway,
she's difficult about what I . . . Blast it, you know
what I mean without saying it!'

'Perhaps I do.'

Bony went with them to the river bank, where he
asked Cosgrove to arrange to have the girl's possessions
collected from the laundry because he might be away
from the house.

Watching them cross the dry bed and climb the
far bank to the horse, Bony found himself wanting
in not having asked why the girl had walked from

Part Two of Jill's Story

Mira and the man had ridden; and while returning to the house he pondered another tiny mystery. In her statement to Constable Lucas the girl had said Lush had abused her before bashing the door with the axe. After she had fired through the door he had been silent. That was singular indeed. Would not his normal reaction to being fired at be to hurl abuse from a safe distance?

Chapter Seven

The Dead Stand Still

When Bony arrived at the house the sun showed it was one hour to noon. Having removed the cases to the laundry, he locked the doors and strolled to the mail-boxes to put questions to the mail driver scheduled to reach them at twelve. The wind had sprung up again, cold and tangy from the far distant Snowy Mountains, and while waiting he walked on farther to note how the track to White Bend veered, as though fearfully, away from the great wilderness of billabongs and dusty declivities called Madman's Bend.

He saw a horseman approaching from out of this bend, and shortly afterwards recognized the Mira overseer, the man who had visited him the previous day. On the pommel of the saddle rested the outward mail-bag. He called to Bony before dismounting.

'Got cold, hasn't it? Hope this easterly won't last.'

His dark eyes were small, and his long face looked a trifle pinched. He was wearing a leather wind-cheater, and the tight trousers tucked into short leggings seemed to Bony the sensible clothes for the time and place.

'It can be unpleasant,' he agreed when Vickory had

52

dismounted. 'It could be less so in the lee of that gum. The mail is more often late than early, I suppose.'

'Tries not to be,' Vickory said, busy with a cigarette. 'After tomorrow he'll have to take the outside track.'

'The men still searching for Lush?'

'Yes, some again in Madman's Bend and others through the top bend beyond the Mira homestead. With no sun even a good man could get bushed in Madman's Bend. About nine square miles.'

'But since Lush disappeared the sun has shone every day.'

'That's so. With the sun he wouldn't bush. Musta fell over into the hole. If he doesn't come up soon he never will.' The overseer drew at his cigarette and thoughtfully regarded Bony. 'There's three no-hopers camped on this side a bit down from our shearing-shed. Just swagmen. Told them about the flood and they seemed surprised it's so close. Nothing else, 'ceptin' a couple of stray horses, and they must have been living off the smell of a gumleaf.'

'The three men you found: how far is their camp from this place?' asked Bony.

'About a mile and a half straight through. Not Lush's type, though. Lush was too flash to clobber with them. He reckoned himself a squatter.'

'Reckoned?'

'Reckoned, yes. He's past tense for sure. I think the mail's coming. On time.'

They could now see the white dust cloud raised by the mail car being swept away westward. Bony continued, 'They tell me that Lush when full never drove faster than ten miles an hour. He was full when he left White Bend Hotel. D'you think that after driving some twenty miles at ten miles an hour he would then be drunk enough to walk over this cliff?'

'Not drunk enough – angry enough,' said Vickory. 'He was a smarmy bloke. Spoke soft and polite, drunk or sober, to men. But under it he stank. He was sober enough when he took to a milk cow with a shovel 'cos she swished her tail in his face. One of our riders happened to see him. He was still bashing the cow when she was dead. Happened, too, with a trotter he raced in town. Backed him all he could and didn't even get a place. Took him to the races in a float: drove him back that fast and that long the horse was never any good afterward.'

'What has this to do with his disappearing into the hole?'

'What I'm getting at is this. Lush gets here in the middle of the night, runs out of petrol, loses his block, rushes to his mail-box and drags out one of the legs, and belts at the utility. Leg breaks and so he goes for another, and in blind rage misses the box and takes a header over the bank. Easy done. The night was as black as the ace of spades.'

The oncoming mail car was not unlike a laden black beetle.

'An interesting supposition,' Bony said without levity. 'Anything to support it?'

'There were four legs to the box. Now there's three. There's a dent on top of the near-side fender that he could have made with the leg. Pity there's no leg or part of one to prove it. Still, when it broke he could have flung it yards in his temper.'

Bony felt like complimenting Vickory on having argued so well when the heavy vehicle was braked

54

to a halt. The red-headed youth leaned out from the driving-seat and said, 'Lush turned up yet, Vic?'

He had no passengers. He took the Mira bag as the overseer answered, and gave out the inward mail-bag. When Bony approached he asked whether he was Inspector Bonaparte, and casually asked, 'Found neither hair nor hide of Lush, eh? Musta done a get after bashing up his wife, and now she's dead he won't stop going.'

'When you arrived here and found the utility, was anyone waiting with the Mira mail?' asked Bony.

'Yes. Ray Cosgrove was waiting.'

'You looked into the utility?'

'Too right! Then I looked around for Lush.'

'Was there anything on the utility, anything on the driver's seat? Purchases?'

'Only an empty beer carton on the passenger's end of the driver's seat.'

'A carton which takes a dozen bottles?'

'That's so. There was a bit of wood on the fender, and when I saw a dent near by I wondered if that wood had anything to do with it.'

'Did it look like one of the box legs?' asked Vickory.

'Could have been, Vic,' replied the driver. 'Could at that. A leg missing, like?'

'Yes. I've been telling the Inspector I reckon Lush lost his block when he ran out of petrol and took to the ute with a leg from his own box. What d'you reckon?'

'Well, someone told me . . . I can't remember who it was now. Anyhow, someone told me that when Lush began to climb a wall he'd go up ten or twelve feet. Take a bit of believin', though.'

'The feller who told you that could have something,' said the overseer, pleased by his own deductions.

'Yair, I suppose he could have. Now, it's me for the track. See you later! Hell! Not here, look like! Next trip down I'll have to take the outside track, and leave the mail at Murramundi. You can get down to Murramundi, and they can get it over by wire, can't they?'

'They can get it over to our side, but we could be cut off by what I hear of the water coming down.'

'Yair, you might have to raise them levees around the joint, Vic. Have a good time. Hope it don't rain on my run.'

'Would you deliver this letter to Constable Lucas, or to his wife?' asked Bony, proffering the letter.

The driver grinned, 'Too right, Inspector,' he assented. 'Always keep sweet with the police's been my motto for years. I'll see he gets it.'

The engine roared, the wheels skidded, and redhead drove off with the careless abandon of youth.

'Levees?' questioned Bony, and the overseer said that during the great '25 flood Mira had had to build a levee to enclose the entire homestead, adding, 'She came that high the water nearly got to Madden's house. This time it could go in and stay in for a week. I'll get going. Have to meet the gang for lunch. We'll come for the cows in the morning. Don't let the chooks out of the yard, 'cos we'll have to snaffle them as well as the dogs. And what about you?'

'I'll leave at the same time,' replied Bony.

With this they parted, Bony going back to the house to take his lunch.

By three o'clock he had satisfied himself that the box leg, or any part of it, was not floating on the surface of the great hole to provide support for the theory that Lush had fallen into it and drowned. Twenty minutes later he was standing on the river bank opposite the Mira homestead.

He could now see the commodious house dwarfed by date-palms and surrounded by a high wood fence, with the offices and workshops to the right. Immediately opposite were the men's quarters, the reservoir tanks on the usual high stands, and the wood-fired boiler on chocked wheels to work the pumps. It was a fine homestead ably supported by the original leasehold, and now too good for the greatly reduced acreage. Down-river were the shearing- and woolsheds, and at a fire outside the shearing-shed two men sat and smoked. The entire area was higher than the bank Bony was traversing.

Now and then he had to turn away to pass a water gutter which would admit flood water to the billabongs lying amid the box-trees and arboreal rubbish covering this enormous bend. The strong easterly wind moaned through the branches of the majestic red-gums. Major Mitchell and black cockatoos chattered at his passing, but only once did a kookaburra chuckle at him. It was four o'clock and the sun was westering when he came to the camp of the three men reported by the overseer. It was deserted.

As was to be expected of these wandering men who work as seldom as possible and cadge food from station cooks, their camp was littered by wind-blown newspaper, mutton bones, and tins tossed into a hole. The mound of ash spoke of the length of their sojourn, and the temperature of the ash proved they had departed that day, obviously decided by the overseer's warning.

57

Bony gave half an hour to poking the paper litter with a stick, but found nothing of interest. He delved into the ashes with the stick, found nothing of interest there either, and then proceeded to cross this Madman's Bend.

It was impossible to maintain a direct route because of steep-sided gutters and soak-holes and the masses of tree debris piled against obstacles by past floods. He cut the tracks of horses, probably of those ridden by the searchers after Lush. He crossed the tracks of two men where it was impossible to detect whether they were going to or returning from the mail-boxes. He caught sight of a wind-quickened piece of paper and plucked it from a bush.

It was a torn shred of tissue paper, and on smoothing it flat he saw the letters *el* against the ragged right margin. The paper was unweathered, and he spent a little time searching for the counterpart. He thought it possible that it had been brought from Mira by the vagrant wind, which could carry such a wisp high above the trees and deposit it in this wilderness.

Resting on a log and making a cigarette, he recalled that when leaving the deserted camp he had reacted adversely to this vast area enclosed on three sides by the river. The overseer had said it covered something like nine square miles, five and a half thousand acres.

Now Bony surveyed what he could see of it: the gnarled grey and red box-gums leaning at grotesque angles, their branches ugly and twisted, their leaves dry and grey-green; the stiff, brittle remains of long-dead bushes; and the ground covering of burr all dead and seemingly malignant. It had no positive attributes. It was neither desert nor jungle, neither flat nor hill, neither verdant nor arid, neither light nor dark.

Light! That was it. He recalled how, when he was leaving the camp on the bank beneath the kingly red-gums, the sunlight had appeared to diminish, and he remembered how he had looked up, faintly expecting to see a cloud masking the sun. There were no clouds, and the sun, now midway down the western arc of the sky, was bright and fell slantingly upon him; yet this world of dusty death and decay intermixed with tortured life had begun to disturb this man of two races before he himself realized it. Feeling a distinct revulsion to the place, he stood abruptly and hurried onward.

The ground was of hard clay rubble, exceptionally bad for tracking, even of horses; the tracks of these he cut but seldom, and he was impatient of being even momentarily interested. He felt eyes watching him, and knew that the old enemy ever lurking in the subconscious once again threatened to ride him like an old man of the sea.

The wind moaned high among the scattered trees, but the air about him was still and cold. In summer it could be still and dehydrating, and a man could lose mental balance, panic, and never be found again.

The ghosts of his mother's people watched him. The same ghosts urged him to run. Resisting the impulse to look back over a shoulder, resisting the command to run, he looked determinedly over the ground before his advancing feet for human tracks, until he came to a tall, slender leopard-wood tree and could see the ground changing imperceptibly from ashen grey to warm off-white.

There was a red-box tree, and there a green wait-abit bush, and over there the avenue of river gums. The sun was before him, and the sun took on added brilliance, and once again he was walking in broad daylight, and behind him were left for the nonce the ghosts of his Aboriginal forebears.

The easterly wind came along the empty bed of the river to sting his right ear and cheek as he passed the mail-boxes. It played with the light-grey powdered surface of the track, and about the boxes. If it had been as strong as this on the night Lush vanished, it was no wonder the man's tracks could not be found.

The dogs were vociferous in their welcome and anxiety for freedom. The roosters chortled at him, and as he passed the birds' dinner-perch to split wood for the stove, the first of the kookaburras landed on it.

Chapter Eight

A Pleasant Conference

Bony and the dogs were in the warm living-room, and all was well with their limited world. Outside the stars were hard and brilliant, and, although the wind kept teasing the stolid red-gums, the sand of the eastern plains – which the hot summer wind from the west would whip into a sandstorm – lay cold and still.

During a momentary lull both dogs stood and growled, and in the buffeting that followed the approaching vehicle seemed to arrive with a rush. Bony opened the door, the dogs rushed out, and Constable Lucas shouted, 'Hope the stove's red hot.'

He was wearing his uniform greatcoat over civilian clothes, and he stamped his feet on the linoleum. He looked cold, and smiled broadly when he saw Bony at the stove. The dogs, now needing no urging, followed him in before he could close the door.

'You had dinner before you left?' asked Bony.

'As you said, yes. I left after dark. I've brought bread and a pound or two of cooked ham.'

'Good! I'm out of bread, and the meat is short. We can eat when we wish to. I felt it was necessary for us to confer, aside from the food supply.' Bony put before the policeman jugs containing coffee and hot milk. 'I've reached the conviction that Lush is not lying doggo somewhere with a bottle or two, and with the river coming down I shall have to work to another plan.'

Lucas opened a parcel to disclose a small, attractive cake which he said his wife had sent, and Bony produced a knife with which to cut it.

'You will not forget to thank Mrs Lucas. News from Bourke?'

'Yes. Following the report on the autopsy a warrant was issued for the arrest of William Lush. The coroner's inquest was held and adjourned. Mrs Lush was buried at five, and the daughter left with the Cosgroves shortly after six. And I telephoned Roger's Crossing, sixty miles south of Bourke, and they say the head of the flood passed them at two o'clock this afternoon. It'll be here tomorrow late.'

'What did you get on Lush?'

Lucas produced a slim notebook and thumbed the pages before replying.

'I gained a pretty good picture, Inspector, being armed with the information about the warrant. People liked the Maddens, and weren't backward in giving information. I tackled the two Roberts men. I told them it would be advisable to speak up, and then asked them if Lush owed them money. They said he owed a betting debt of sixty-odd pounds, and that he still owed the balance of a hundred and eighty-five pounds on the trotting horse he bought from them last year. It appears they heard of Lush driving the horse home after the races and permanently crippling it, making it worthless. They had threatened to sue if the two debts weren't cleared within a week. That was ten days ago, and they started proceedings when Lush said he couldn't fork out.

'The store account stands at two hundred pounds odd, but this has always been taken care of by the wool cheque and concerns the Selection. The hotel is personal. Lush owes fifteen-pounds-something there, and the publican wasn't particularly anxious because Lush had owed much more in the past.'

'Thus three hundred pounds would have been more than adequate to square his debts,' Bony observed.

'Then I inquired what Lush had purchased that day, since the mail driver said he saw only an empty beer carton on the utility. The store people say he bought nothing there. The publican says he left at close-up time with three bottles of whisky and six of beer in a beer carton. The baker told me he had got six of bread, and that he had supplied Mrs Lush with bread since her first husband died.'

'So it would be possible for Lush to live on bread and booze for three full days,' commented Bony.

Lucas pursed his lips, saying, 'Possible, but I doubt Lush would make his supplies last that time.'

'I do, too. Did you question the mail driver on the points mentioned in my letter?'

'Yes. There was no bag in the Madden's box, and we took on the inward one he left, remember. Told me he had been questioned by you, and then said he'd been thinking of the dent on the front mud-guard, thinks he can remember it wasn't done a century ago. The piece of timber lying on the mud-guard could have come from the mail-box. He said he didn't bother with it. He was positive there was no bread and that the beer carton was empty.'

63

'A casual young man,' Bony said. 'Get his statement?'

'Most of them are out here. Yes, he made a statement. There was the other point you wanted cleared up, the one about who, and how often, waited to take the mail from him. The drill for all these wayside deliveries is that the people have to leave their outward bags in the boxes, even if there is no mail to send out. He takes these bags to the post-office at Bourke and White Bend, and the same bags are returned to the same boxes, mail or no mail. When he gets to the boxes here, there's always someone from Mira with their mail-bag and waiting to take the inward – or nearly always, anyway. Because Madden's Selection is so much nearer, quite often there would be no one at the box, because the outward bag could be left before the mail car reached it and the inward bag picked up at any time.'

'The important part of the drill conforming to postal rules is to have the outward bag at the boxes for the driver to carry on to the respective post-office.'

'That's so,' replied Lucas.

'And on the morning the driver found the abandoned utility there was no outward bag in the Madden box.'

'We now know why.'

'We think we know why,' Bony said, and began the manufacture of another cigarette. 'This morning the Mira overseer brought the mail to the box. He had an interesting theory to account for the damaged mudguard.'

'I heard part of it from the mail driver,' Lucas said, and then slowly went on, 'I don't know that I have a clear idea.'

'I am beginning to suspect there is some connection between what happened to that utility and to Lush,' Bony said, regarding the constable with puckered eyes. 'I asked young Cosgrove what he thought might have happened to Lush, and he said that, having run out of petrol just where the ute did, Lush got out and in the dark wandered over the cliff. The fact that the headlights were off when the mailman arrived could mean that, realizing he was stranded, Lush switched them off, then got to ground and missed direction in the dark and so walked over the cliff.

'Vickory the overseer goes a few steps farther. He pictures Lush getting to ground in a rage and rushing to the mail-box for a piece of timber with which to take it out on the utility. Lush gives it a heck of a crack, the stick breaks, he flings the stick away and, rushing again to the mail-box in the dark, misses it and so goes over the cliff. Now, can you visualize Lush switching off his lights before rushing to the box for a leg?'

'A bit hard to see that,' Lucas admitted.

'The lights were switched off, according to Cosgrove, and if Lucas, having broken the first leg, went to the box for the second and then fell over the cliff with the lights still on, who switched them off?'

Lucas shrugged.

'Then the mail driver remembers seeing a part of the box lying on the damaged mudguard, and this supports Vickory's theory, and in part supports Cosgrove's opinion. Therefore we find a modicum of agreement between these three men.

'In her statement to you Jill Madden said she returned home to find her mother badly injured and her stepfather absent, and that she hadn't since seen

65

him. That ties in with the theory that he walked or fell over the cliff and was drowned. When I taxed her about the door and the bullet hole in the ceiling she added much to what you took down. She admitted she sat up waiting for Lush to return, that she had locked the doors and windows, and that if he broke in she was determined to protect herself and her mother by shooting him.'

'You could be getting to some place by going round in a circle, Inspector.'

'Possibly, and please don't call me Inspector when we are alone. My friends call me Bony. I probed into this second edition of the girl's story, and she said that Lush came to the locked door, was refused admittance and began to scream abuse. Still refused, he went to the woodheap for the axe and proceeded to bash the door down. She fired a warning shot at the ceiling and, when he would not desist, she fired a shot at the axe-head which protruded through the door. After that shot there was not a sound from Lush, and she expected to find him dead when she opened the door at daybreak. He wasn't there, and he wasn't asleep in one of the out-buildings. If we are to believe that Lush wasn't killed, then can you picture him being stunned to silence by the shot through the door, and not continuing his defiance and abuse. The natural reaction to the shot would be to retire hastily and shout defiance. And if Lush had lost control of himself, as he is supposed to have done by attacking the utility, he wouldn't have cleared out but would have gone on bashing at the door and yelling abuse – or wrecked a window.

'There is another angle, too,' Bony went on. 'I am unable to see Lush leaving his attack on the door and returning to the derelict utility, if he did return to it, without taking with him a can of petrol to bring the ute home. Can you?'

'Having got home he would have cooled down about the stranding, but he would have come to the boil again when the girl fired through the door, and he could have forgotten to take petrol back to the ute,' argued Lucas.

'You offer another supposition which increases the fog,' Bony said. 'It is a good one, too, although on examination I am doubtful of it. However, we'll look at it further. We concede that in his rage he forgot to take petrol, that on returning to the ute he realized he had forgotten the petrol, and boiled over again and rushed for the box leg. Having turned off the headlights, he didn't think to turn them on again to enable him to see what part of the vehicle to bash with it.'

Constable Lucas stared at the table lamp, then said, 'Did Jill Madden say why she had not mentioned the door in her statement to me?'

'She did. Her mother was alive the next morning and begged her to burn the door in case someone saw it and scandal broke out. When you took her statement she was too upset by the death of her mother to think of the door. I was present, you will remember, and I am sure she was really upset, and had reason to be so.'

'Proper fog over Madden's Selection, isn't it?'

'So dense that I intend to transfer to Mira homestead and carry on from there.' Bony rose and brought the coffee from the stove and filled the cups. He smiled at the policeman, his blue eyes seemingly very dark in the lamplight, and glinting with yellow lights. 'This case delights me, Lucas. What at first appeared superficial now has depths as deep and as dark as the bottom of that bend hole.'

Lucas combed his fair hair with his fingers, and, returning Bony's smile, looked much younger than his thirty-odd years.

'Vickory told me there were three tramps camped on the river bank below the shearing-shed on this side. Would you know anything of them?'

'No, Inspector.' Bony frowned, and Lucas chuckled. 'Suits me, Bony. You don't look like an inspector any more than I look like a Roman Emperor. But the Super told me of your record, and it's mighty decent of you not to wear the braided hat.'

'Oh, I can when I'm so minded,' said Bony, laughing. 'My career has been highlighted by so many successes that I have to practise humility to retain mental balance. Let's sup on some of that ham. Fire up the stove.'

Having set the table, Bony was slicing bread when he asked, 'Any of the men at Mira ever given trouble?'

'Nothing serious. Most of them get a bit rowdy when they're in town. Even young Cosgrove had to be locked up to cool off. No charge, though. Sorry for himself when loosed the next morning. Funny how drink affects men. Mr MacCurdle becomes dumb. Young Cosgrove sings at the top of his voice. Feller named Grogan wants to fight, and he can't fight his way out of a paper bag, and everyone knows it, including him. They're not a vicious bunch.'

'What is your opinion of Mrs Cosgrove?'

'Is the boss, with everyone knowing that, too,' replied Lucas. 'MacCurdle is supposed to manage the place, but she manages him. Vickory is supposed to overseer the men, and he does that. But Mrs Cosgrove, I'm told, does the hiring and the sacking. Has the reputation of feeding the men well, giving them spells in return for extra work, but work they have to when she wants it that way.'

'And the relationship between her and the son?'

Lucas chuckled. 'According to the wife, Mrs Cosgrove thinks the sun shines on him. Believes there will be no woman good enough for him to marry, and therefore intends he won't marry. Keeps him short of money, considering the money she has tied into Mira and what her husband made in his time.'

'Plenty of money?'

'More money than the Queen,' replied Lucas without disrespect.

Chapter Nine

Unusual Characters

Bony was at breakfast when Mrs Cosgrove phoned him.

'Good morning, Inspector Bonaparte. How are you?'

'Well, thank you, Mrs Cosgrove. How did your visit to Bourke turn out?'

'No incident on the road, but it was a tiring journey – my son had to go very wide of the river, there and back. I've been telephoning northern neighbours about the flood, and they estimate it will reach us not later than six tonight. Have you any plans?'

'Yes, I would very much like you to invite me to stay at Mira for a few days. I would try to be as little trouble as possible.'

Bony fancied that Mrs Cosgrove hesitated before saying, 'Of course, Inspector. We shall be delighted. I am sending the men for Jill Madden's things, and the cows and dogs and fowls. They could collect your case, too. What have you been doing these cold days?'

'Oh, milking the cows, feeding the chooks and the kookaburras,' Bony lightly replied. Then, abruptly serious, he went on, 'The death of Mrs Lush brings

70

her husband's disappearance into the realms of
homicide. That means I shall have to continue looking for him.'

'It is dreadful, isn't it? Poor woman! What she put
up with makes my blood boil. Jill told us about it.
She will be coming with the men to make a final
check and lock everything up.'

'Very well, I'll leave my case with hers as I may
not be here. The cows are still near the shed, and
the chooks I've kept in their yard. The dogs, of
course, will be chained.'

'You are a man of many parts, Inspector,' Mrs
Cosgrove said. 'I've been talking about you with
Superintendent Macey, and it appears you are quite
famous in police circles. Anyway, I shall be looking
forward to your stay with us.'

After thanking her, Bony replaced the receiver,
and went out to hang on the line the bedsheets he
had used and washed. Finally he put sandwiches and
a bottle of cold tea in a sugar-bag which could be
slung from the shoulder by a rope handle, gave the
remainder of the food to the dogs, and departed.

The morning promised a better day than the previous one. The wind still lay to the east, but was
much less strong, and Bony could feel the warmth of
the sun as it travelled south from the northern
hemisphere.

Coming once again to the mail-boxes, he paid
particular attention to the remaining three legs of
the Madden box. A fifty-pound wooden tea-chest with
its open end to the east, it rested on a square frame
of three-by-three-inch milled timber; this was supported at each corner by a leg of two-by-two-inch
milled timber. The entire arrangement had been

71

painted inside and out, and now needed repainting. The legs having been sunk into the ground, the remaining three still gave the box stability.

Testing the legs of the Madden box, Bony found it would not need much effort to tear a leg from it. With one hand against the corner of the box, he was confident he could wrench the leg off with the other, and when he examined the place where the missing leg had rested he found the part buried in the ground still there, its severed end showing the ravages of white ants.

In a state of uncontrollable rage Lush could have wrenched the leg free. Having done so he would have had to take eight steps to bring the leg down upon the upper curve of the mudguard. The blow was sufficient to dent the guard and to snap off the end protruding beyond the apex of the convex shape, the tensile strength of the wood having been reduced by the termites.

Then what had he done? According to the overseer's theory, he had flung away the piece of timber in his hand and rushed back to the box for another leg, missed the box in the dark and so gone over the cliff. Where was the broken leg? Bony had circled the place to find it and to pick up betraying tracks. He had looked over the waterhole and the flanking rock ledge for it.

Lush's reputation certainly supported the overseer's deduction from the material facts, but from the same facts, based on the missing box leg, an equally plausible theory could be built – namely that Lush had been met by someone when he returned to the utility with a can of petrol; there had been a struggle, Lush had wrenched away the leg to attack or to defend

72

himself, and had either slipped over the cliff or been thrown over.

Both these theories could contain the truth, but Bony had relegated them to the sphere of remote possibility in favour of the probability that Jill Madden's bullet, fired through the door, had killed Lush and that she had disposed of the body.

She had admitted to taking the damaged door to the fireplace at the killing-yard and there burning it. Bony had seen at the side of the house a light iron wheelbarrow, and he had seen its marks on the path from the killing-yard to the house when he and Ray Cosgrove had looked for Lush, and again when Jill and Ray had been with him the preceding day. The barrow was obviously used to transport carcasses from the yard to the house, but it could also have been used to transport Lush to the killing-yard, from which place it would have been no great task to get him down the bank to the small but very deep river hole from which the homestead water supply was raised. There would be no tainting of the house water, which came from rain-tanks.

Bony had made his visit the previous day to the camp of the three dead-beats on the river bank below the Mira homestead because, although their camp was nearly two miles from the abandoned utility, they could not be discarded as possible participants in Lush's disappearance. This Darling River, sometimes called the Gutter of Australia, had once been notorious for scoundrels living in secret camps deep in its great bends, men who would lie in wait for travellers on direct tracks, and either lure them from the road or kill them and convey their bodies into the waste to dispose of them. One or more or these three men could have seen the abandoned utility before Cosgrove had done so.

This was yet another possibility, with the probability still manifest, the only certainty being the water advancing down the river to fill over all the bend holes, to flood into all the bends, to cut off Madden's homestead, and drive Bony to the Mira homestead on the far side. He who loved time because time was ever his ally seemed now about to be deserted by it.

Picking up his lunch-bag, he walked on down to the lower level bordering the outside verge of Madman's Bend, and then turned into it to come again to the leopard-wood tree that he had been so glad to see.

Every man has to live with himself, and Bony was not going to be constantly reminded of having been afraid of this waste to the point of fearing being afraid of it. From here in he followed wide zigzagging lines in the hunt for evidence that a man or men on foot had recently emerged from the area.

He saw a diamond snake sluggishly crossing a patch of wind-collected leaves. He saw a goanna lying along the dead branch of a tree, and the reptile looked down upon him with black and brilliant eyes filled with hate, occasionally thrusting out its forked tongue, seemingly as a threat. He heard a goat bleating and another answering, but they were unseen. Once he thought he could hear a bell rhythmically tolling a tinny note, and he judged it to be hung from the neck of another goat gone wild, or even a cow. But mostly it was silence about him, a silence having no association with the whispering of the slight wind passing the grotesque and shapeless trees.

74

Whether it was because he was concentrating on the job, or because the sunlight now was stronger and more golden, or because he was unconsciously refusing to think of the unknown which brought fear, today he experienced no spiritual influence directed by his maternal progenitors. Now grim in determination, he trudged on and on, evading fallen trees, skirting deep gutters, crossing shallow billabongs, yet always following his zigzagging lines over a general course deeper and deeper into the great bend.

He was sitting on a log and smoking a cigarette, and thinking he would go no farther, when the back of his head and neck was touched by a thousand cold but gentle pin-pricks. He swung about, and saw nothing but the haunting face of desolation. It was then that he experienced a tingling in the soles of his feet, rising up about them to his ankles, and he stood and moved his toes. These physical sensations had alaways given him warning of danger.

Inspector Napoleon Bonaparte was smitten by fear, and the man known to his countless friends as Bony bit his nether lip as he waited, taut as a violin string, for the danger to make its origin known.

It began to do so a moment later. There reached Bony an unnameable sound, low and distant, not unlike sea waves crashing against rocks, not too fantastically unlike a great organ so far away or so buried in stone that only the deepest note carried to his straining ears. What a place! What an evil place was this dry, dirty, terrible waste!

From the cadaverous trunk of a leaning box-tree emerged the shape of a man. He was a very tall man. He was dressed in old trousers and was wearing a tattered green overcoat. He was bearded, and his grey hair draggled beneath the rim of his battered felt hat.

Advancing towards Bony, who stood feeling the pins-and-needles in his feet and neck subsiding, the man placed his feet as though sleep-walking. Bony could not see his eyes: they were directed downward. In one hand this apparition carried a billycan, and resting on the rump of his buttocks was the usual cylindrical swag or blanket roll, the top of which was higher than the hat.

'Bomb . . . Bomb . . . Bomb.'

These repeated sounds coincided with the man's tread. A few moments later they were repeated, and were followed by varying notes which ultimately made a tune or melody. The man was loudly humming a tune to which his feet kept time, and when he was fifty yards off Bony recognized the tune. It was the Dead March in 'Saul'.

Bony had encountered many characters, and had heard of many others: men who have tramped up and down the rivers, year in and year out, men who have begun as station hands and old-time blade-shearers, and gradually drifted into wanderers living on handouts from station kitchens. They have but one thing in common. They are always on the move, always going somewhere beyond the next bend, always on a journey without end.

This one slowly advanced towards Bony, humming his tune, keeping his gaze to the ground. Eventually it became clear that he was unaware of Bony and was about to pass him by.

'Good day!' Bony greeted him. The humming ceased. The character neither halted nor looked at Bony. Bony heard the phrase repeated several times as the character moved on beyond him: 'I'm dead. I'm dead.'

'I am beginning to think we both are,' Bony called after him, and then began to pity this human wreck. For sure he wouldn't go far today at his present speed, and this thought led Bony to estimate the fellow's course. He had come from the trees to the south-west, and was headed to the north-east: towards Mira homestead.

The character might not know of the coming flood, the head of which was due at Mira about six o'clock. The sun said it was now close to eleven, giving five minutes either way. It was difficult to calculate the distance to the homestead, for Bony had zigzagged so much; he could make only a rough guess that it was between one and a half and two miles. A smart walker can cover three miles per hour, but this old man at his present speed would cover only a quarter-mile in the hour, and, if he was two miles from Mira, then he would need eight hours to arrive there. And the flood was due in seven.

It was not to be presumed that the flood water would come with a rush. It would be days before the water covered this bend area, and hours before it began to flow into the gutters and deeper billabongs. The danger lay in being unable to cross to Mira, and in the water flow being too fast and too loaded with debris for a boat to be paddled over it to pick up the derelict.

Bony decided to go after the man and hurry him along. He stood, and was about to snatch up his gunny-sack when he heard shouting beyond the point where he had first seen the hummer. The shouting halted him, and when again it reached him he was

77

sure the shouter was coming from the south-west on the track of the hummer.

Bony waited, and presently saw a man moving across in front of him, betraying the fact that he wasn't tracking the hummer but anticipating the hummer's objective. Bony shouted. The second man saw him, and turned to meet him.

He was short and rotund, and his face and everything about him suggested the curve, whereas the hummer suggested the perpendicular line. He also carried a swag and a billycan, and in the billycan a black and white kitten. His blue eyes were anxious as he said, 'Good day-ee, mate! Happen to see a tall bloke?'

'Yes. He just passed me. Humming the Dead March.'

'Good-oh! We was having a bit of shut-eye, and when I woke up he'd skipped. Bloody rotten country to look for a looney in. 'Course he ain't looney all the time, but when he is I got to look after him sort of. How far's he ahead?'

'See that tree?' Bony asked and pointed. 'We could see him were it not for that tree.'

The faded blue eyes in the whiskery face showed relief.

'I'd better get going, mate. Old Dead March Harry and me been mates for ten-eleven years. Not a bad poor bastard, y'know, but he gets to worrying me sometimes. See you at Mira, perhaps.'

'You are aware that the river is coming down a banker?'

'Too right. It's why we're headed for Mira direct. The mail driver told us about the flood being due to hit Mira at six. Well, so long, mate. See you some time! Hooroo!'

Chapter Ten

A Set-Back for Bony

Three hours after the appearance of Dead March Harry and his buddy, Bony retreated from Madman's Bend, satisfied that he could do no more, and happy to be out of it.

As expected, he found the house locked and the homestead stock removed. The wheelbarrow was not in its accustomed place, and, as even the woodheap axe had vanished, he was confident that it had been locked into the detached laundry. Its mark along the path to the killing-yard was partially wiped out by the boots of the evacuation party.

While Bony sat on the river bank above the small holes of water, there was about him, beneath or beyond the occasional chortle of a kookaburra and the chattering of distant galahs, the silence of the deserted homestead. The absence of sound always to be associated with a homestead prompted the thought: Why did a man build himself a house on land likely to be surrounded by water?

An answer came readily enough. Why build a house away out on the wind-swept, sun-scorched western plain? Suffering isolation or being forced to retreat once in every decade was a small price to pay

79

to live beside this river, insultingly named a gutter, a river infinitely more beautiful than Australia's largest river, the Murray.

Sitting here, relaxed and intentionally permitting his mind to wander, this product of two races felt the stirring of the urge to walkabout which often took his mother's people from a river like this out on to the dry and hot plain, there to starve and thirst, and to return gaunt but glad to be back at home under the red-gums. Walkabout! What had he been doing since early morning? Ah, but then it was not the same as surrendering to the siren call luring a man to a sand dune merely to gaze over its far slopes.

The stirring of the urge to walkabout was probably the result of his having actually achieved nothing throughout the four days he had been engaged on this Lush case. He had got nowhere, and he was now becoming impatient at having stood still so long.

Abruptly realizing what was happening, he took himself in hand, knowing quite well that his long list of successes was based on the rock-firm attribute of patience.

Alive, William Lush might be apprehended; might even surrender to the police. Dead, it was only remotely likely that his body would ever be found, because for Lush the grave-digger would be this river, soon to flow and spread for miles either side, but slowly to recede, leaving for months a million stagnant little lakes and pools. If Lush were dead, if the river buried him for ever, there could be no proof that he was dead; the evidence proving that he had fallen over the cliff when enraged, or that he had been killed by another man, would also be taken care of by the river. Thus it was that this man of two races, this complex man who could admit to no failures as a man-hunter, could anticipate failure – the one thing that could destroy pride in himself and bring him down to the level of his maternal ancestors with their constant urge to go walkabout.

Anticipation of failure, however, was the trap set for him now, as often it had been. Patience was the staff with which to prod the trap to harmless iron, and patience was the rapier with which to slay failure. He would cling to this case for years if necessary. He could hold to it like a tiger cat, and be deaf to the yells and screams of his superiors recalling him from it, superiors who thought he should be another Holmlock Shears and complete a case in five minutes with a report of five thousand words.

Bony suddenly burst into laughter at the thought of Holmlock Shears crawling about this river with its Madman's Bends, and studying it with his glass. Still chuckling, the depression vanquished, he crossed the short distance from the killing-yard and the carcass gallows, and fell to studying the bank from it to the waterhole.

He satisfied himself that no object, such as a body, had been dragged down the steep bank, but he could not be sure a body hadn't been rolled down it like a log. There was a narrow path running diagonally down the bank from the yard to the waterhole, this having been used but seldom, and then for the probable purpose of attending to the pump. On this he found a print of a boot, but its details were insufficient to tell him the size of the boot which made it more than four days ago.

Between the hole and base of the bank lay a flatbottom boat. It had been so long out of water that its

seams were parted. As it was bottom up, Bony turned
it over, shrugged, and walked round the rocky lip of
the hole.

Into the hole went the wood skids down which to
lower the pump. He could see the pump six feet
below the surface. He could not see the bottom, but
could see curving dark patches betraying heavy tree
branches resting on others, if not on the bottom. He
could find no sign that anyone had been to this hole
since William Lush had abused his stepdaughter on
being refused admittance to the house.

. Deciding to make yet another examination of the
great hole below the mail-boxes, he sauntered along
the dry bed, the avenue of gums standing high and
trying to reach each other above him. The sun was
westering and the trees to his right cast their shadows
across the rock bars and the stones which the river had
rolled and rolled for miles to make them round before
laying them as cobbled ways. The crevices were filled
with the red sand carried by the wind from the plains,
but on reaching the bed at the boxes the river's own
sand was piled into a long thrusting spit, deep and
loose and off-white, covered with unrecognizable
tracks.

Bony spent a full hour going over the ground
already examined with the thoroughness that marked
all his investigations. He achieved nothing, but he
saw something that made him stare intently up-
river.

The reach extended above the Madden homestead
and turned sharply to the east. At this bend there
appeared a disturbance similar to that made by a
snake actively crossing a bed of long-dead leaves. Continuing to concentrate on the place, at least one-third

of a mile distant, Bony watched the 'bed of leaves' grow thick and thicker still, and lengthen from bank to bank as it appeared to slide over the river bed towards him.

Glancing at the sun, he found that time had sped, that it was almost five o'clock. The head of the flood was less than half a mile from him, and one hour before its estimated time.

Tramping over the sand spit, he thought of Dead March Harry and the short fat man, and inwardly expressed the hope that they had not relied on the time estimate; then, climbing the bank opposite the boxes, he once again reviewed his fruitless efforts to trace William Lush.

Now on the bank he watched the head of the flood. There was nothing spectacular about it, merely a carpet of leaves and debris carried by a low water surge. Just below Madden's homestead the carpet appeared rapidly to thicken, rumple, break into separate pieces; and these moved faster until they rejoined and the carpet was relaid.

When it had come to within a hundred yards of where Bony stood the front edge was halted – by what he could not determine – and from it water gushed in foam and came on free of debris. Behind it further debris was added to the mass, which again piled upon itself until the pressure broke it into smaller masses of leaves and bark streamers and small branches. Thus the river methodically built its dams and destroyed them, the water not deeper than fifteen inches.

Bony watched the debris swept to the edge of the great hole and carried swiftly across it, portions being caught by the rock ledge, teased and torn away. The placid sheet of water vanished, and the broken masses moved round the bed into the reach above Mira, to rejoin and roll on to smother the dry, flat bed.

The water was the colour of putty. For a time it carried merely light debris and the pronged branches which were rolled by the shallow water, over and endlessly over, like buckbush quickened by the wind. Bony was so interested that when again he gazed up-river he was astounded to see a wall built of heavier branches being thrust forward, rolled forward, branches which ceaselessly rose to lift high, sodden streamers of bark like a desperate man tossing up arms heavily loaded with seaweed.

This barrier was at least twelve feet high, and a man caught in it would be mangled, crushed, and minced. It rolled past Bony into the once placid hole, sank as though in a quicksand, came up and floated on till caught by the shallow bed and again brought to its rolling movement.

A tree fallen down the left bank and the protruding roots of another on the opposite bank caught both ends of the roller, bringing it to a halt. Behind it the water could actually be seen rising against it, and the free floating branches and tree trunks which moved relentlessly past Bony swiftly became lethargic and were gently pressed against the barrier, thickening it and apparently strengthening it.

Before it passed Bony the water had been only knee-high; now behind it the water rose to the height of a man, and swiftly to the height of two men; and its height, which in passing had been but twelve feet, rose swiftly to fifteen, eighteen, twenty feet.

Fascinated, Bony proceeded along the bank to look directly down upon it. From the lower face water gushed whitely as though through the valves of a man-built dam. He glanced up-river. The stream was rounding the bed ponderously, bearing further trunks and branches, and then he saw the result of the destruction of a similar barrier far up-river. That barrier had freed a great volume of imprisoned water, and the release now appeared in the form of a wave which Bony estimated to be five to six feet high. The wave hit the barrier. The barrier shivered, moaned like a beast in pain, began to scream, and surrendered. It sank, rose, was torn asunder, and torn again until on the racing water the arms of countless branches lifted high their loads of bark and went on racing to the Mira bend like a crowd of infuriated rioters.

Bony sauntered along the bank, still absorbed by this phenomenon created by a rainstorm hundreds of miles away. Although the river would fall and rise and so on, it might be many years before it ceased to flow. Now with its burden of harvested debris it was sullenly alive, brown in colour, ugly in its triumph.

On reaching the upper extremity of the Mira Station bend Bony could see the homestead, and he paused to regard it from the edge of a deep water gutter extending into a shapeless billabong. To the left was the fine house surrounded by the garden enclosed by a wooden fence. Opposite Bony stood the steam engine to power the pump raising water to the high tanks. To the right of this were the men's quarters, and half a mile down-river were the shearing-shed and the woolshed.

A sheep bleated. Magpies chortled and cockatoos cawed. They flew over him, and looking up he saw that they were black cockatoos, birds larger than a crow and as black, except for the under wings, which were blood-red. A dog barked. A man laughed. The cook came from his kitchen to twirl an iron bar round and round the inside of an iron triangle.

It was the right time of day for a hungry man to visit Mira.

Chapter Eleven

Introduction to Mira

'Government House' at Mira Station was entirely fitted to be the governing centre of a million-acre property. It was built on a knoll well back from the billabong at which Bony had stopped to survey the entire homestead. Of Colonial design, it contained a dozen bedrooms, a ballroom and a drawing-room almost as large. The verandas were twelve feet broad, and wire-netted against flies and mosquitoes. The surrounding garden guaranteed shelter from the cold winter easterlies, and cool protection from hot summer westerlies. It was the kind of home associated in literature with wealth, service, gracious living, security.

Naturally, when Mira's million acres and its eighty thousand sheep were reduced by seventy-five per cent, the service staff as well as the employees had to be reduced, if not by seventy-five per cent, then by sixty. Mrs Cosgrove still maintained a house staff consisting of an excellent cook, two maids, a yardman, and a kitchen maid. To comparative poverty she had conceded formal dinner dress, and this well pleased Bony, who was travelling light but managed a dark-blue lounge suit. Lastly, Mrs Cosgrove maintained all her old love of table appointments and service.

Raymond Cosgrove occupied the head of the long table, his mother seated at his right with Mr Mac-Curdle next to her, and Bony on his left with Jill Madden next to him. Again naturally, the conversation was limited to the one topic of the flood.

'I suppose, Mac, you had the boats brought up from the water,' Mrs Cosgrove said, with no hint of doubt in her rather hard voice.

'I did that, Mrs Cosgrove,' replied the manager. His thin hair was as sandy as his moustache, clipped like a soldier's. He had once been built like a soldier, too, but at fifty he was soft and inclined to paunchiness. 'It could be months before the river will be well enough to put them back again.'

'Not soon enough for me,' remarked Ray Cosgrove. 'I'd prefer to row a boat to the mail-box than walk or ride. Tough going up, but drifting down a silvery river suits me. Besides, there's always the chance of hooking a fish on a spinner.'

His mother regarded him dotingly with eyes of dark grey, the most attractive feature of her broad face. To Bony she said, 'Ray is always hopeful of beating Jill's father, who hooked a twenty-pound bream.' Turning to her son, she added, 'There won't be any fishing now for many weeks, and you or someone will have to ride down to Murramundi. And we'll have to do with two mails a week, not three: it might even be one.'

'Does the river rise fast?' asked Bony.

'No, not as fast as some northern creeks run,' young Cosgrove told him. 'Take a week for it to get really high. You see, all the way down there's billabongs and channels and small lakes to fill. The last time it covered all of Madman's Bend, for instance.' He reddened faintly, and laughed. 'So I was told by my

88

father. Before my time, you know. Anyway, we'll get it this time. That was when the levee was built. We'll have to look to that, Inspector. Are you an expert with a shovel?'

Bony laughed, saying, 'I anticipated that question.' To Jill Madden, who had not yet spoken a word, he said, 'Your kookaburras will be waiting dinner. Did you tame them like that?'

She nodded, and refrained from speaking, keeping her face tilted.

Ray persisted, 'You will have to do something, Inspector.'

'I shall probe, I shall question. I shall observe, and perhaps criticize.'

'Every man to his last, is that it?'

'It is a sound philosophy.' Bony smiled blandly. 'You know, if we had Superintendent Macey, my State Commissioner, my immediate superior, and two or three others I have in mind, all here with us, I would support strongly what is implied by your question concerning a shovel. I can foresee that they are going to be extremely impatient with me, and if they were manhandling shovels they wouldn't have time to think of me.'

'Why impatient with you, Inspector Bonaparte?' asked Mrs Cosgrove.

'They will be saying that that feller Bonaparte is lolling around Mira and looking at the stars and things instead of reporting back and getting on with this or that investigation which has baffled their best men. They will be howling at my heels because I haven't apprehended William Lush and am not on my way back to headquarters.'

'Do you hope to locate him now that the river's

down in flood?' asked Mrs Cosgrove, and Bony felt rather than saw Jill Madden raise her head as though the better to hear his reply.

'I permit myself to hope he is still alive, and that I shall apprehend him. If he is not alive, then I shall continue to hope I shall eventually apprehend the person who killed him.'

'But, alive or dead, he's on the far side of the river, and you won't get across now for perhaps several weeks,' argued young Cosgrove.

'Then the river will fall and I shall cross in one of the boats.' Bony airily waved a hand. 'Time! What is time? Tomorrow, next week, next month, even next year will not worry me as it will worry my superiors. I've been sacked a dozen times for closing my mind to an order to return, and always I've been reinstated. However, be sure I can use a shovel in a crisis.'

'Well, time is going to worry us, Inspector,' declared Mrs Cosgrove. 'We shall all be very busy, but you must not hesitate to ask your questions, nor to ask for any assistance we can render. The sooner you find Lush, or find out what happened to him, the better for poor Jill. And for us, too. We have a very personal interest, Inspector. Jil''s father and mother were very sound people. Not as affluent as we, but of our standard of behaviour.'

Bony thought that could mean much or little. The use of the word affluent indicated an incomplete acceptance of the Maddens. This woman had set her values when her husband controlled a million acres, and she would doubtless still have those values in her present circumstances. Intuition, rather than anything she said or implied, told Bony that her reaction to him was due to Superintendent Macey.

Introduction to Mira

The Scots manager-accountant stoically regarded the cheese dish, and a moment later Mrs Cosgrove rose saying that she and Jill would retire to the drawing-room. Bony opened the door, and Mrs Cosgrove tilted her face fractionally as she passed from the room. Meanwhile Mr MacCurdle had brought the port and the glasses from the sideboard.

'My mother is a stickler for the rules,' young Cosgrove said, proving that he was perceptive, as Bony had indeed been slightly surprised. 'My dad once told me that my maternal grandfather had been a dean at York Minster, and although he argued that Mira sheep station wasn't York Minster, and he wasn't a dean, anyway, he'd come to agree that the rules were good, especially the rule about the ladies leaving the gents to drink in peace. Here's to the ladies, both of them.'

'And here's to Inspector Bonaparte,' said MacCurdle, swiftly refilling his glass, and then producing a cigar. 'We shall hope that your stay here, Inspector, will be to your likin'.'

'I am sure it will, Mac, if only you and Ray will drop the rank and call me Bony, as my wife and children always do, and my chief does when in a rage with me.'

Cosgrove grinned at the Scotsman.

'We could be breaking a rule, Mac.'

'We could so, Ray.'

Both men looked at Bony, who said, 'Split the difference. When at the table, and when I am hounding you with questions, I am Inspector, and when I am otherwise off duty, I am Bony.'

'Agreed,' Cosgrove said, and MacCurdle nodded.

'Consider a wager?' Bony persisted, and they

91

nodded. 'I bet you both a shilling that Mrs Cosgrove will be calling me Bony at table within a week from tonight.'

MacCurdle frowned, making Bony think that a shilling was too much to risk. He recognized his mistake when the manager said, 'You're a new experience, Bony. I've only been in Australia twenty years, but you are a new experience. What's he to you, Ray?'

'Can't work it out, Mac. There were two chaps at school from Singapore, and I reckon Bony has something we haven't. Look! Time's up. Coffee!'

The description of the Maddens as sound people was, to Bony's mind, applicable also to these two men. However, never trusting first impressions, he put the thought from him as he was served with coffee by Jill Madden. His first impression of the girl and Mrs Cosgrove was wearing fairly well. Environmental changes typed the older woman, for, superimposed on the ecclesiastical education and the influence of cathedral society, was the influence exerted over many years by the broader way of life in the Australian outback. Mrs Cosgrove had been sufficiently intelligent to accept much of Australia while retaining much of England, recognizing that both countries could contribute to the fashioning of this emerging Australian nation.

Many people would hold that to come from England into this back country would mean a severing of cultural ties; but such people would fail to see that the land itself is richly rewarding, and that the wife of a man owning eighty thousand sheep, a fine house, and an estate of one million acres would have a wonderful outlet for attributes that would doubtless be severely limited by a cathedral close. This, Bony considered, explained Mrs Cosgrove's decision to cling to Mira, reduced as it had been, after her husband's death. He knew he would have to tread softly to win the bets he had made with her son and the manager.

As for Jill Madden, she had surprised him when he met her at dinner. She was in evening dress. Her hair was done becomingly, and a little make-up banished the effect of the outdoors. Finding himself now and then being examined by her, he decided she was far more sophisticated than he had supposed and that he would have to deal with her more subtly than hitherto, especially since she would certainly be advised by Ray Cosgrove. Her speech proved the influence exerted by a public school, an expensive item in her father's budget.

The 'polite conversation' was terminated by Mrs Cosgrove's asking the girl to play something, and Bony was astonished when she sat at the baby grand and began Liszt's *Liebestraume* No 3. To Cosgrove he whispered, 'She plays wonderfully. I didn't see a piano in her home.'

'The bastard smashed it last April,' said Cosgrove, and pointedly returned to enjoyment of the music.

The information spoiled Bony's appreciation, and for the remainder of the short session the music was background noise to him. Here was motive enough to kill William Lush, without the addition of the threat of bodily injury. The piano might well have been the last joy in the lives of this girl and her mother. If it may be said that any man was born to be murdered, surely that man was Lush.

Presently Jill Madden left the piano, and excused herself by saying that she was out of mood this evening.

'Of course, Jill, we understand.' Mrs Cosgrove spoke for all of them. 'But you play beautifully. Your touch is like a butterfly: mine is as heavy as a cart-horse. I think we will put Inspector Bonaparte under the bright light, or whatever it is they do with persons they want to question. He says he will be asking us many questions, and I think we should first test him with some of ours. He hasn't said anything of what he has found out: even what he thinks happened to Lush, if anything.'

'Mother, you are brilliant tonight,' said her son, smiling at Bony. 'Inspector, you're on the mat and the light's in your eyes.'

'Well, fire your questions. I may or may not pre-varicate at this beginning of an inquisition.'

'Then tell us, Inspector, what you think happened to Lush,' Mrs Cosgrove persisted.

'I think he vanished.'

'Of course he has vanished,' agreed Mrs Cosgrove, a trifle sharply. 'D'you think he fell over into the water-hole, or just ran off to drink himself into a coma?'

'On what I've heard about him, I hope he fell over the cliff and was drowned.'

'Hoping isn't thinking,' Raymond argued. 'Turn the light on more.'

'Mercy!' moaned Bony. 'No more light. I give up, sarge. I'll confess. I think it probable that he fell into the waterhole. Whether accidentally or whether he was pushed I am unable to say.'

Chapter Twelve

The Swagmen's Retreat

At six o'clock on a July morning the day has barely
opened its eyes, and it is a long wait until breakfast
at seven. Arrayed in a bright-blue dressing gown, with
slippers to match, Bony braved the cold air of the
verandas, as well as Mrs Cosgrove's disapproval, by
prospecting for the kitchen, which he found to be
detached from the house. The open door and the
aroma of coffee gladdened his heart. He called, 'May
I come in?'

'What d'you want?' asked a woman. Stepping inside,
Bony saw her seated at a bench, a small, shrivelled
woman with her grey hair bunched into a bun.

'I would much like to share your teapot,' replied
Bony, and waited hopefully for the invitation. As with
everything else at Mira, it was a very large kitchen,
and in it the small woman seemed like a large
doll.

'You are the new guest,' she said as a statement of
fact. Then, graciously: 'Yes, I suppose you can. Plenty
in it. Help yourself.' Bony helped himself. He would
have liked to warm his back at the rapidly heating
range, but was aware that nothing raises a bush
cook's ire more than a man standing before his

95

range or camp fire. She said, 'There's biscuits in the tin.'

'Thanks. What's your name?'

'Mrs Tanglow. You Inspector Bonaparte?'

'Yes, Mrs Tanglow. It's going to be another fine day, isn't it?'

'My worries if it's fine or wet.' Her brown eyes were screwed to pin-points. 'That right you're lookin' for Bill Lush?'

'Well, I have been. He seems to have disappeared.'

'Hope he stays disappeared. I hope some more he'd walk into my kitchen asking for a cup of tea.'

'Oh, you'd like to see him again?'

'I'll tell you what is no secret,' Mrs Tanglow said. 'My hubby is about twice of you. When we'd been married a week he twisted my arm, and another time he smacked my face. Up to then I was always a lady, you understand. Yes, twice you and a bit. I kicked him in the stomach, and when he was bent over I hit him on the head with the wood back of a dust-pan brush. It didn't hurt him as much as my boot in his stomach, so I hit him twice more to make a proper song and dance of him.'

Mrs Tanglow paused for comment, and Bony was confident he could have picked her off the floor with one hand. He looked his interest, and she said, 'J'you know what, Inspector? My hubby ate out of my hand from that day to this. Only way to fix a bully. Had Mrs Madden returned bash for bash she'd of been alive today.'

'You could be right, Mrs Tanglow.'

'Right! 'Course I'm right. Now you get out of my kitchen. I gotta earn my wages, not being a policeman.

And don't bother to wash your cup and saucer. The help'll do that.'

'Thank you, anyway,' said Bony. 'When I find Mr Lush I'll bring him here for a cup of tea.'

'Do that, and turn your back so's I can put a pinch or two of strychnine in it.'

After this pleasant beginning of the new day Bony showered and dressed, smoked another cigarette, and waited for the breakfast gong. He found young Cosgrove and MacCurdle talking on the veranda overlooking the garden gate, beyond which were the office and store, and the out-buildings. They greeted him as Bony, and led the way to a small room opposite the kitchen where, he was informed, the men always breakfasted.

'Seen the river?' asked the manager-accountant. 'No? A wee bit early, eh? Well, she's half-way to the top.'

'She'll rise slower from now on, Mac,' Cosgrove predicted. 'The higher she gets the slower she'll come, but she'll come high before falling. We're going to inspect the levee. Care to come along?'

'I'd like to, but I have some telephoning to do and,' Bony smiled, 'questions to ask. Where is the telephone?'

'In the office. I'll introduce you to the office.'

Eventually Bony was shown where the keys were kept, and then shown the switchboard. For a while he stood on the office veranda, feeling the warmth of the sun, and watching the two men departing in a utility. He waited until eight before ringing through to Constable Lucas.

'You remember the statement from the mail driver?' he asked.

'Yes, of course.'

'Did he mention meeting and stopping to warn two men about the flood?'

'No, his statement concerns the utility, time he arrived at the boxes, and meeting young Cosgrove.'

'Then when he is again in your town, please get from him a second statement to include who and what vehicles, if any, he met with on the morning that Lush disappeared.'

'I'll do that,' Lucas promised. 'How high is the river?'

'Half-way up the banks, I'm told. I haven't seen it this morning. Saw it beginning to flow yesterday. It was an hour early, and I was nearly caught on the Madden side. In Madman's Bend I encountered two characters: one called Dead March Harry, and the other was his mate. Didn't get this second man's name. Know anything of them?'

Lucas chuckled. 'Oh yes! Given no trouble, though. Dead March Harry and Mick the Warder have been on tramp together for years. They work sometimes, but not long at any job. Harry is harmless, and Mick looks after him. Their beat is from Bourke down to Wentworth. I don't know what truth there's in it, but I was told that the small feller was a warder in the Victoria Department. Difficult to believe it, a warder coming down to being a swagman.'

'Well, they were the pair who told me the mail driver told them about the flood. They said they didn't know the flood was so near. It occurred to me that the driver could have met other swagmen, or travellers, that morning Lush disappeared. We think that young Cosgrove was the first to find the abandoned ute. Someone else could have been there before him.'

'I'll check. What next?'

'That's all. The routine alert for Lush would have gone out to all police stations when the warrant of arrest was issued, but we could take the additional step of alerting every homestead within a radius of a hundred miles. Will you see to it?'

'Of course. You believe he cleared right away?'

'No, I don't believe so, but I've no proof that he didn't.'

Bony rang off and after delay contacted Superintendent Macey.

'Morning, Super. You located Lush yet?'

'Why bother, Bony. You're on his tail . . . I hope.' Macey's voice was deep. 'Having a nice holiday?'

'Wonderful, Super, wonderful. Thank you for putting me on the right side of my hostess.'

'We've known her for several years. Tough outside, generous inside. Are you encouraged?'

'By the job, no. Actually I rang you to say not to bother me if I'm here for a year.'

'That bad, eh! Well, I know you, my obstinate friend. I'll cushion you against the thuds from your H.Q.; that is, as much as I can. Flood passed you yet?'

'Arrived yesterday. That correct it will be a record?'

'Near record, anyway. O.K. Keep in touch. We'll keep tag on Lush here, and I'll let you know if we dig up anything about him before he worked for Mrs Madden.'

Bony locked the office and replaced the keys where MacCurdle kept them, strolled outside the house fence, skirted the vegetable garden and continued beside the levee which now hugged the river bank. Not having been needed for many years, it was weathered and in places reduced by two to three feet from its original height.

Coming opposite the men's quarters and cookhouse, he could see up the long reach to the bend on which the mail-boxes stood. It was too far to pick them out from the background. He watched the dun-coloured water bearing parts of trees, branches, and small masses of debris, noting how the water boiled when flowing over the concealed bend hole, and how it appeared to be loath to pass by the billabong extending to the house garden and round into the maze of the low land beyond. The river would have to rise another twelve to fifteen feet before it would flood into that area.

Beyond the men's quarters he found several men working in and about what appeared to be a machinery shed, and, seeing the overseer with them, he crossed to find out what they were doing.

'You appear to be busy,' he said to the long-faced Vickory.

'Getting things ready if we have to raise the levee,' replied the overseer. 'Haven't noticed Lush floating down yet.'

'You still think he fell over the cliff?'

Vickory nodded. He was going over the treads of a caterpillar tractor, a young man assisting him. 'About time Lush came up. Three days, isn't it?'

'That is the general guess. No one looking for him now?'

'No. All hands wanted here. You any good with a scoop?'

Bony chuckled, saying, 'I have been asked if I am good with a shovel. I shall leave the scooping to one more experienced.'

Two other men under the direction of a third were servicing a bulldozer standing beside a front-end loader, and Bony was aware that this equipment would have been employed in excavating surface dams, and cleaning out dams already sunk. Now it would be ideal for work on the levee.

Leaving the men, he sauntered farther along the inside of the levee and so to the workshed, beyond which was the shearing-shed. The first was locked. Between the front of the second and the levee several men were squatting or standing about a fireplace. Two he came to recognize as Dead March Harry and Mick the Warder. Coolly, a shade insolently, Bony looked from one to the others, counting eight. To Mick the Warder he said, 'The river beat itself by an hour. You and your mate could have been caught.'

The rotund man grinned and his eyes were calculating. Dead March Harry was sitting on a case and moodily looking into the fire.

'Never trust the river,' he said. 'We crossed over a good two hours before she came down. Were you lookin' for Lush, too?'

'Trying to pick up his tracks. No go.'

'They reckon he fell into the hole by the boxes. Good job if he did.'

'Why so?' asked Bony, sitting on a vacant case and rolling a cigarette. They eyed his clothes, his shoes. A large, greying man replied for Mick.

'A flash, mean cove, Lush. A worker come up to be a squatter. Them sort are worse than the real squatters what will give a swagman a go. The Cosgroves'll hand out a bit of tucker, but the likes of Lush wouldn't give away the smell of an oil-rag. Won't be no loss if he got himself drowned.'

For a little while they discussed William Lush's shortcomings, and from the general conversation Bony learned that the missing man came from Cunnamulla, just over the border in Queensland.

'How long ago would that be?' he asked, and was told away back in 'fifty-five, an additional item of information being added by a man with stiffly upright white hair and clipped white moustache: 'Lush's father was the publican at the Black Cockatoo. Old Lush took a dose of cyanide in 'fifty-seven, so someone told me. Could have been that young Bill tickled the till too much. He managed a selection for his old man after he left school.'

Bony did not divert the conversation from pubs and publicans, which engrossed the company for twenty minutes, but when he stood to leave a man asked what job he had on Mira.

'I'm staying on holiday,' he replied, and laughed. 'Already been asked if I could use a shovel or a bulldozer. Could have to use one or other at that, by all accounts of the coming flood.'

'Might want us to work,' a little runt of a man asked in broad West Country accent.

'Too right, Jacko. You better get going,' he was advised, amid general laughter.

Bony was hoping to withdraw without disclosing his occupation – not that it was important – but Mick the Warder tackled him.

'What d'you do for a crust?'

'I'm a Queensland detective inspector,' he replied. 'As I told you, on holiday.'

The gathering froze into silent stares, and the silence was broken by the rotund mate of Dead March Harry.

'Look us over, Inspector. See our crimes on every dial. Look at poor Old Jacko. Got a record as long as your arm. Look at me. Bumped off more blokes than you got fingers to your hands. Anyway, you did us a good turn yesterday.'

'I don't agree. I would have gone after your mate if you hadn't turned up, knowing about the flood. Well, see you all some time.'

'You will. Better stay here and work, if we have to, than get caught some place without nothing to eat and smoke.'

Chapter Thirteen

Bony Charms Mrs Cosgrove

For an hour Bony rubber-necked the servicing of the machinery, and when the morning smoko gong was sounded he accompanied Vickory.

'At the shearing-shed camp I found eight men. Some time later would you see if the three camped on the other side of the river are among them?' he requested.

'Yes, they're there,' Vickory said. 'I looked the lot over first thing.'

'I suppose all the swagmen and others on the river will now be congregating at safe station homesteads?'

'All barring the hundred per cent ratbags. They'll manage on bardee grubs and goannas and things.'

'Men like Dead March Harry?'

'Oh, he's not nutty all the time. His mate looks after him. They work on Mira now and then. Harry was a big-gun shearer with the blades, and then with the machines before the war. Quite a handy man on the place, but too unreliable unless watched. Which is why Mick the Warder has to be employed with him. There's no knowing when he'll go into his Dead March act.'

'Then Mira will have a labour pool?'

Vickory smiled a little sourly, saying, 'That's so.'

'Could you supply me with the names they answer to?'

The overseer gave the names, which Bony noted on the back of a letter. Later Bony saw the overseer proceed to a small cottage where clothes hung on a line, and, some of the items being feminine, he guessed that Vickory lived there with his wife. He was sure of it when a small child came round the house to meet Vickory and be taken up.

The office being open, Bony entered and found Mrs Cosgrove working on a typewriter; he would have withdrawn had she not called to him to stay.

'You have been to see the river, I suppose. Looks nasty, doesn't it? Glad you came. I've been wanting to talk with you.'

She was wearing a gingham house frock, and now her eyes were a darker grey than when he had seen them in the drawing-room the previous evening. Her voice was harder, too.

'Firstly, what can we do for you to make you comfortable?'

'Nothing whatsoever. Your hospitality is perfect. However, there is something you might be able to do for me. Off the outside office – I assume this is the inner one – I observed another, a small room. Might I use that? You see, I may have to interview men and obtain statements from them.'

'Oh, certainly, Inspector. It would be more convenient for everyone than having them in the house. It's furnished. In fact, Mr MacCurdle uses it for relaxation.'

'Thank you. I'll try to avoid inconveniencing Mr MacCurdle.'

Mrs Cosgrove smiled, and for the first time Bony

saw a woman rather than one wearing a male mask. He found himself being studied, and Mrs Cosgrove, realizing what she was doing, bit her under-lip and hastened to explain.

'I'm being rude, Inspector. Forgive me. You see, Superintendent Macey and his wife have been close friends of mine for several years. We gossiped about you the other day. He told me of your remarkable career, and I've been finding it difficult to associate one of your abilities with you in person. My understanding, through plays and novels, of police inspectors has been to build them into a class widely apart from ordinary men. There I go again. Making another *faux pas.*'

'But you don't, I assure you. Police inspectors are a class apart from ordinary men. I know. I've associated with them for several decades. They know everything. They command expert organizations. And often they fail. It happens, because I make no claim, that I am an ordinary man, and nothing like an inspector in a police force. You should hear what my Chief Commissioner says about me as a policeman.'

Mrs Cosgrove rather liked the beaming smile; the reserve with which she had met him, and which had continued till then, melted away. His eyes opened, and she was caught in the net which had ensnared so many. It was only for a moment, and she was unsure that she had felt what she thought she had experienced.

'I can recall the early period of my career,' he was saying, 'when I was very conceited and given to boasting. Then I came to understand that one's attributes are not things one has manufactured oneself, but inherited gifts. I inherited certain gifts from my father, and also I've inherited gifts from my mother and her race. Now inspectors are what we may call lop-sided. What attributes they possess have been handed down to them by only one race. Thus, by comparison with me, they are placed at a great disadvantage.'

'Inspector Bonaparte, you are making fun of me.'

'I may be exaggerating just a little, but I am not making fun,' he said, laughter about his mobile mouth. 'Now where is this tête-à-tête taking us? Did we not begin by discussing police inspectors? Yes, we did, I remember. Let us be frank. You are mystified by my official rank, and I believe you would in future find no difficulty in clarifying your foggy picture of your guest could you keep in mind what I've said about inspectors and forget I am one. All my friends call me Bony. Could we not be friends?'

Mrs Cosgrove burst into laughter, and Bony said as though pained, 'Now you are making fun of me.'

'But I'm not. I am only beginning to understand what Tom Macey said of you. Yes, we are going to be friends. But please don't expect me to understand you all at once. This sounds like Ray and Mac returning, and it's time for morning tea.'

Over the teacups and buttered scones Ray and the manager gave Mrs Cosgrove their report on the levee, enumerating points at which work should begin; she produced a sheet on which she had typed the river heights at numerous points upstream during the major flood of 1925, and, against these figures, river levels she had obtained this morning. Her son and MacCurdle examined the data, and the younger man agreed with the manager when he said that the present threat might not be as great as it had been in that far past year.

'What you think could be so,' she said briskly. 'My husband told me that the greatest danger from the river was at the section opposite the reach to the mail-boxes, because if the wind blows a gale from the west it creates waves to pound against the levee as well as to raise the mean height of the water.'

The subject occupied them for some time; when they had finished Bony asked Raymond Cosgrove to accompany him to his 'office'.

'Your mother has kindly granted me the use of this room, Ray,' he explained after closing the door. 'There are matters I want to clarify, and I am sure you can assist me. We'll do it by question and answer, and put the result into a form of statement.'

'Go ahead, old pard.' Cosgrove smiled, then frowned. 'But are you still keeping dark what Jill said about shooting through the door, and her burning it?'

'Certainly. I trust you haven't mentioned it to anyone? Actually you should not have been present. I permitted it because I felt that you thought a great deal of Jill.'

'I do, too. All right, let me help as much as I can.'

'Give the average number of trips, say, covering this month, you made to the mail-box.'

It pleased Bony that Cosgrove was cautious, for it proved his earnestness.

'Six days a week: I'd say I took the mail four days a week. Old Mac likes the walk now and then.'

'Thank you. Now relax and cast your mind back to the trip you made when you discovered Lush's utility. What time was it when you left here?'

'For the downward mail it's never later than a quarter past eleven. That gives spare time to meet the mail.'

'That morning you would pass along the garden fence, cross the billabong and so gain the river bank and follow that? Right?' Raymond nodded. 'Other than men working normally, did you see anyone, meet anyone?'

'No.'

'Did you hear anything unusual?'

'No, I can't say that I did.'

'So, having come opposite the boxes, you went down the easier slope to the sand spit, skirted the waterhole and climbed up the opposite bank. You then saw the utility?'

'I saw it before I made the crossing.'

'On reaching the boxes, just what did you do?'

'I remember standing at the box and looking round for Lush. There was no sign of him, and I thought he must have run out of juice and walked on home. Only half a mile or less. Then I remembered it was gone half past eleven, and reckoned he must be suffering from a bender, or was too damn tired to bring petrol to get the ute home. That made me check the dash gauge by switching the ignition. The tank was empty.'

'Did you think to look about for tracks?'

'What d'you think? There's the ute and there's Lush's home. Anyway, it was a windy day, and the ground there is of fine tilth, easily blown off by the wind. No, I never thought to track.'

'You said, I think, that the headlights were not on. What did you do after checking the petrol tank? Think hard.'

'Well, I saw the beer carton on the seat, and I reached in to see what it contained, and there was nothing. That surprised me somewhat because it wouldn't have been there unless it had contained bottles. Then I argued that Lush had transferred the bottles to a sack he'd probably have in the back to save his trousers if he had to make a wheel change, and it would be easier carrying the bottles home in a bag than in the carton. I was certain this was what he'd done because the passenger door wasn't shut.'

'The door nearest the empty carton?'

'That's it, Bony.' After further urging Cosgrove said, 'When young Tolley came with the mail car I gave him our bag and took over the inward one. To save him getting out, he asked me to get the Madden bag, and I went there and found the box empty. Tolley had passengers, and he and I talked about the ute, and about Lush having gone home and stayed there.'

'Did the driver mention having met a car or truck before arriving at the boxes that morning?'

'No. Why?'

'On present knowledge you were the first person to see the utility after Lush abandoned it. That was at eleven-forty, or forty-five. Quite late in the day.'

'I see the drift, Inspector. But there could have been a car or something which came south before I got to the boxes and met the mail car.'

'I have considered the possibility,' Bony gravely admitted.

'I am interested in what became of six bottles of beer and three bottles of whisky known to have been in the carton when Lush left White Bend. Let us now examine your theory of what happened to Lush, expressed that morning you came to Mrs Madden's house and found me there. You said you thought that Lush had fallen over the cliff. Subsequently, Vickory told me he thought Lush had lost his temper with the utility, pulled a leg off the mail-box and attacked the vehicle. The leg broke and he rushed for another, missed the box in the dark and so ran over the cliff. Had you mentioned your theory to Vickory?'

'Yes, the same day.'

'Didn't you see that one of the box legs was missing?'

'No. I was too interested in the ute.'

'Didn't you notice a piece of the box leg lying on the front guard?'

'I don't remember seeing it. If I did it had no significance for me.'

'What d'you think of Vickory's theory?'

'It could have happened, but we know it didn't happen when the ute blew out on him, but could have when he went back to it with petrol.'

Bony paused in the interrogation while he rolled a cigarette. Then he said, 'I would be inclined to agree with Vickory were it not impossible for Lush to take petrol to the utility in his pocket. He must have taken petrol in a can, and the can would have been with or near the abandoned vehicle. It wasn't.'

Chapter Fourteen

Facts Are Lacking

When Bony again saw the river he could not tell by how much it had risen since early that morning. It bore much less flotsam, however, and the boiling action over the great hole at this Mira bend was much reduced. Its speed was about the same, but, as he had been informed, it would gradually become slower as the lakes and billabongs and creeks lower down filled, and the general course would be broadened at places for miles.

Sitting on the levee, he watched the Gutter of Australia in process of becoming unrecognizable as a river. He noticed how at the edge of the bank above the bend the current tended to flow in reverse to the main stream and, watching a piece of wood, saw that the reverse current there was distinctly strong. Ray Cosgrove had not been wrong in saying that against a fast river it wasn't hard to row a boat upstream to the mail-boxes by keeping close to the bank.

A beautiful river, Bony thought. A unique river indeed. A river with a personality that captivated men like Dead March Harry and his friend Mick the Warder, and those others camped at the shearing-shed. A kindly river, offering so much in wood for the camp fire, in shade from the sun, in fish for the hungry. The ugly bend country was at odds with it, outside the pale marked by the avenue of stately and ancient red-gums nearly two thousand miles in length.

A tractor engine roared in the direction of the machinery shed, and Bony remembered that he was supposed to be working and not mooning and crooning over the Darling River. The wind was lower to-day, and its subdued singing in the trees was the lullaby accompanying an action scene of nature which had strange effects. Bony wanted to lie full length in a boat and go drifting on and on watching the trees flow by.

Sauntering on the top of the levee, he skirted the shallow billabong and so came to the gate at the lower end of the garden. Here he found thriving citrus trees and rows of grape-vines, and in a canegrass summer house he found Jill Madden with her sewing-basket.

'May I sit with you?' he asked, and she regarded him solemnly with her large black eyes until her mouth broke into a hesitant smile.

'Mrs Cosgrove said this is her "thinking house", and that I could come here when I wanted to think and be quiet.'

'In that case I won't disturb you,' he said, and made to withdraw.

'Oh, don't go, Inspector. I didn't mean that.'

'Thank you, Jill. Meditation is always helpful, but you should not have much to meditate upon. Your mother's tragedy is yours, of course. But you're a young woman, and all life is before you. Life is a journey, don't you think? We set out, and eventually we arrive at the end of it: some sooner than others. And on the journey we meet other travellers and have our little adventures, and difficulties and triumphs. Have you decided what you are going to do – which road to take from the junction you have come to?'

The girl shook her head and bent her face over the material on which she was working. She said, 'I've been living with Lush for years and years. Not really for years, though. Only two, since Father died. But it seems years and years, and living with Father was in a life before. I was sixteen when Father died, and I had to come home from school. I was nearing eighteen when Mother married Lush. As Mrs Cosgrove said, I've never had any playtime. Father was going to send me on a trip round the world, and instead I came home and milked the cows and tended the sheep and helped at the shearing. No, I haven't decided what I am going to do.'

The girl was wearing a pretty blue frock, and while rolling a cigarette Bony recalled her as he had first seen her: in rough trousers and riding-boots and a faded blouse. She was speaking like a woman much older, but then two years with Lush would age any woman.

'What's going to happen to your sheep?' he asked. 'They haven't been shorn yet, have they?'

'They were to be shorn next month. Vosper, who has a place out west, is taking them to his shed and looking after them. That's my trouble, Inspector. I can't live at home and I can't go on living here, can I?'

'I don't see why not.'

'That's what Mrs Cosgrove said. She said it would take time to settle matters. You know, proving the will and all that. And the flood will delay things, and sort of keep me a prisoner here.'

'Quite a nice prison, anyway, Jill. Then there is Ray.'

'Ray's more trouble.' Jill sighed audibly. 'He wants to tell his mother about us and marry me, but I know Mrs Cosgrove won't agree to that, and I feel . . . I feel . . . I feel I am living here under false pretences, if you know what I mean.'

'Well, I wouldn't let that disturb you for a little while, the circumstances being what they are. You are really in love?'

Jill nodded, and kept her head bent over her work.

'Then there is the probability that in time Mrs Cosgrove will come to change her mind about it. By the way, do you know how the property was left by your father?'

'He left it to Mother in trust for me.'

'Therefore Lush hasn't an interest?'

'No. He thought he would take it all over, and didn't know the truth until after he married Mother. It was one reason he treated her like he did. Mother said she didn't think to tell him before they were married.'

'Then that clarifies the situation, Jill. You are the sole mistress of Madden's Selection. Unless, of course, your mother by will made Lush your guardian.'

The girl was silent for several minutes, and when she spoke her voice was so low that Bony had to make the effort to hear.

'That's what she did, Inspector. Appointed Lush my guardian.'

'When did you know this?' he asked.

'Several months ago. I tried to get Mother to have it altered. She said she would the next time she could get Lush to take her to Bourke and the solicitor. But he wouldn't agree. You see, poor Mother was frightened of him, and ever so weak.'

'I'm sure all that could be changed now that Lush is wanted for killing your mother, Jill – that at the moment you are, in fact if not in law until Lush is found to be alive, your own mistress.'

'It's what Mrs Cosgrove said, Inspector. And we don't know if Lush is alive or dead.'

'That's for me to find out. It's why, incidentally, I want to ask more questions. What d'you really think? Is he dead or alive at this moment?'

'I believe he's alive,' she replied, still softly, still keeping her head bent over her sewing. He asked her why she believed this, and she continued, 'He wasn't outside the door that morning. He wasn't in the men's hut, or in the shed, or anywhere. Ray's sure he fell into the bend hole. I don't think he did, knowing Lush.'

'How so?'

'He was always too careful of himself. Wouldn't drive fast when he was drunk. There was that time when two swagmen came asking for meat, and Lush went out and abused them. One of them was a big strong man, and he grabbed Lush by the shirt and shook him and Lush cringed and kept silent. He was like that when I shot through the door. Not a word out of him.'

'What you say is interesting,' Bony admitted, thinking that his surmise on this particular point was illogical. 'How long ago was it that Lush abused the swagmen?'

'Oh, weeks ago. About Easter, I think.'

'Did you know them?'

'No, but Lush did. He threatened to have them

116

arrested. To us women, of course. He said then that one was called Wally Watts, and the other Miner Smith.'

'Did they come again?'

Jill shook her head, and Bony looked at the list given by Vickory. The name Watts was there. Again he probed. 'Do you know or have you ever heard of a man called Dead March Harry?'

'Everyone knows Dead March Harry, Inspector. He's been up and down the river for years. Has a mate they call Mick the Warder.'

'I met them. When did they call in for tucker the last time?'

'The day before Lush went to town. No. It was two days before Lush went to town. I was out on the run, and Mother told me they'd been. Lush was away, too. Fishing at a bend up-river. He liked fishing. Poor Mother was always generous to Dead March Harry, and Harry always returned her kindness by chopping wood and bringing it to the living-room door. None of the others did – the regulars, I mean.'

'None of the regulars appeared about this time?'

'No. There aren't so many as years ago, according to Mother.'

Bony fell to meditating, and presently the girl asked what he was thinking about.

'About nothing in particular,' he confessed. 'Just darting from one subject to another, and so on. You know, Jill, I am coming to think that you could be right that Lush is alive. Your story of the abused swagmen shaking him and deflating him like a punctured tyre supports your other story that he said not a word after you fired through the door. He knew he had severely maltreated your mother, and then realized you had taken the stand you did in determination to keep him out for good. I could agree with you were it not for many faults in the picture of that night. Who owned the utility?'

'It belonged to the Selection.'

'There's plenty of petrol in the machinery shed, and he could have filled the tank and taken an additional supply, and cleared out with the vehicle. He didn't know how desperately injured your mother was, and the risk of being apprehended for stealing the utility would be very small. However, he didn't take the vehicle, and he didn't have any of his own property save what he stood up in. The motive we consider could have been his does not stand up.

'The theory that he returned to the utility and somehow in darkness fell over the cliff is very weak. The place wasn't strange to him. Even if another theory is examined – that he lost his temper and attacked the utility – it is made very weak by the same argument, that Lush knew the place and would be consciously aware of the cliff. Now the facts as you have told them concerning his attempt to break in do strongly support yet another theory. Obviously you won't like it.'

'All right, Inspector. What is it?'

'That when you fired through the door the bullet killed him. Then, or when day broke, you found him dead outside, and you, with or without assistance, took the body on the barrow and dumped it into the waterhole below the house. It was then essential to destroy the damaged door, which was done by burning.'

Jill Madden's reaction to this theory was unexpected. Slowly she removed the material and needle from her lap and placed them on the bench beside

her. Slowly she stood, and slowly turned to face Bony,
who also stood. There was neither fear nor resentment
in her wide eyes when she said, spacing the words,
'That is exactly what I would have done had I killed
him.' The dark eyes narrowed when she frowned.
'How did you guess that, Inspector? As I sat up the
rest of the night I believed I had shot him, and I
planned what you said I did when day broke. Mother
hurt and crying in the bedroom was the last straw.
The range fire went out and the room got very cold,
but it wasn't the cold freezing my mind. Yes, that is
exactly what I would have done if I had found Lush
dead outside the door. You must believe that because
it's true.'

'Let us sit again, Jill.' Putting a hand on her arm,
Bony urged her to sit before saying, 'We were going
over several theories, were we not? Beliefs or dis-
beliefs must not be permitted. When investigating a
crime one usually begins on the premiss that the
crime has been committed. There may be reasons,
however, merely to assume that a crime was committed, and in the case of Lush we have reason
enough to assume he was killed. In what I've just
said, belief or otherwise is of no importance. Only
facts are important.

'Your story of having barred Lush from the house
is supported by the change of the door and its
destruction by fire. What you found on opening the
door, if anything, and what you did subsequently
isn't supported by a single fact. Between that back
door and the laundry is a cement path, and if Lush
had been shot and only wounded he would have shed
blood on that path, and you could have washed off
the blood. I took samples of the soil from either side

of the path, and analysis may indicate the presence of blood. Then there is the wheelbarrow. If Lush was killed, then even the passage of several hours would not prevent the body exuding blood, and here I am sure that the barrow does not contain such a sign because it has not been washed for a considerable period.

'I am being patient, Jill, when telling you all this. Facts, not belief, are what is needed. I am permitted to hope. I hope you did not kill Lush. I hope his body may be found, but think, not believe, it may never be. I hope he is still alive, but think he may be dead. I think it possible that you conveyed his body to the river, but I have found not a single fact to prove it. There are our theories, with not a fact to support one of them.'

'Then what will you do? What shall I do?'

'I shall go on meanderingly looking for facts. You will stay here at Mira, be patient, be grateful for the kindness extended by Mrs Cosgrove, and the love given you by her son. And now we may admit to beliefs. You may believe that every cloud has a silver lining, and I may believe that the disappearance of William Lush will one day be cleared up. Smile, Jill, just a little.'

Jill looked at him with misty eyes, and, instead of smiling, burst into sobbing.

Chapter Fifteen

A Ship for the Crows

Bony was relieved to hear the men's cook sounding the afternoon smoko call, and, thinking that sympathy would prolong her sobbing, he chided the girl. When she had removed the traces of weeping from her face they proceeded to the little room for afternoon tea. Here they found Mr MacCurdle and Mrs Cosgrove.

'We have been meditating in your "thinking house",' Bony said lightly. 'A peaceful retreat in which to relax. Have you any startling news of the flood?'

'Nothing of the flood, Inspector. You are asked to ring back Constable Lucas. We have been planning our defences.'

'You sound like a chief of staff, Mrs Cosgrove.'

'I have to be both chief of staff and general officer, Inspector. Mira will soon become besieged by an enemy, and tomorrow we begin to throw up the earth works. If you don't want to be beleaguered you should withdraw tomorrow.'

Bony smiled his bland counter.

'Only if you command my withdrawal, *mon général*. Otherwise I elect to stay and work on a shovel or a bulldozer. Is the airstrip outside or inside the levee? I omitted to notice.'

'Inside, Inspector. The only other way out remaining to you is by horse down to the point opposite Murrimundi homestead, and crossing the river by holding to the mail wire. From there you can get to White Bend without much trouble, but from White Bend it would be a long way round to reach Bourke.'

'I shall stay. I shall never again fly with Doctor Leveska.'

'Well, the only other airman to get you out is Father Savery, and they do say he is worse than the doctor.'

'How they go on living is a mystery,' said the manager.

'There's no mystery about them,' Mrs Cosgrove said, a shade sharply. 'Alcohol saves the one, and prayer saves the other. And what we would do without either of them I don't know. Now we'll check on the wool in the shed. Coming, Jill? And you, Inspector?'

The girl said she would like to go to her room, but Bony accepted, and the manager drove him to the woolshed in a powerful utility. Here stood a stack of filled bales, and here Mrs Cosgrove decided that the bales would have to be restacked above reach of the water should the levee be broached.

'We'll put those loafers to work in the morning, Mac. You can oversee them.'

'Very well, but don't you think you could leave them to me?' expostulated the manager.

'Why? They're no difficulty to me.'

'There's still time enough for them to withdraw from the fortress. We should take them gently.'

'Gently? Bosh! I know how to deal with working men.'

MacCurdle shrugged and, with Bony, accompanied Mrs Cosgrove to the group of men – ten in all – gathered about their fire.

'Good afternoon, Harry. Mick! And you others. Some of you have worked on Mira before,' she began, and Bony thought it a good beginning, 'and you should know the latest about the flood. We are going to be cut off, perhaps for a week, perhaps a month. Those of you who don't want to be cut off had better leave at once. If you stay you will want food. I want men. Those who will work will report to the cook for breakfast, and then to Mr MacCurdle to go on the books. Those who stay and won't work – well, they tell me there are goannas and snakes in plentiful supply.'

'Me and Mick will be reporting for work, ma'am,' said Dead March Harry, from whom the despondency of the morning had departed.

'I think I'll be packing up,' voted the shrimp of a man called Jacko. 'I ain't cut out for hard labour.'

'You can boil a billy, surely?' said Mrs Cosgrove.

'Too right, I c'd do that.'

'Very well, you can off-side the cook.'

A large red-headed man flexed his arms and said, 'What about starting work right now, Mrs Cosgrove? Me, I'm tired of looking at these blokes, and we're out of yarns, anyway. Besides, most of us has run out of tobacco.'

Mrs Cosgrove glanced at the manager, and Mac-Curdle shrugged. Mrs Cosgrove looked pensively at the gang, knowing that some were hopeless until brought to desperation, and that others genuinely needed employment.

'Very well. Mr MacCurdle will put you on. Jacko, you tell the cook how many extra he will have, and to set you to work. That'll be all.'

Motioning to Bony to accompany her, and leaving the utility with the manager, Mrs Cosgrove crossed to the levee and looked at the river. Bony stood beside her, saying nothing. Eventually she turned towards the sheltered house and proceeded along the levee.

Here the river came round the Mira bend like the rim of a gigantic wheel, the light-brown surface disturbed only by the expanding discs thrust upward by ponderous power. The wind had died away. There was nothing of turbulence, and yet nothing of gentleness in the flow. It was not unlike tarnished gold on its way to distant moulds, and the odd pieces of flotsam seemed to be partially buried in half-solid matter.

'It looks bilious, doesn't it?' Mrs Cosgrove remarked.

'It would not inspire our great Australian poets, but it will eventually, when the sediment has cleared. You've seen it like this many times?'

'Many times during the years I've lived here, Bony. How I hated it, and how I have come to love it!' Mrs Cosgrove laughed softly. 'There, you see proof of it. I find no difficulty in calling you Bony, because I have lost my English reserve and you are indubitably part of this land.'

'If you give Australia the chance it will certainly captivate you,' Bony said. 'I've encountered many who admit first to hating it and then to loving it. You came here shortly after the war, I think you said?'

'Yes. My husband was in the Air Force. What he saw in me I don't know. I was everything he was not. He was gay and casual and impudent, and a tilter at windmills. I detested him. Repeatedly I told him so, but we were married by the archbishop in my cathedral. Then we came out to Mira, and the river I had heard rapturously described was barely running in a ditch, and I loathed it so much I wouldn't look at it for a year.'

'Then the river made itself heard.'

'Yes. How did you know?'

'It has a voice, a little voice to whisper to you, a mighty voice to shout at you.'

Mrs Cosgrove halted and turned to regard Bony with quizzing eyes. She said, 'You spoke of poets, remember. You could be one yourself. Yes, I heard the river shouting at me, and I hated it. The wild westerlies would blow when the world was filled with the shouting of the trees. My husband then had a fast motor-boat, and one evening he induced me to go with him up the river. The day had been hot, and the evening was cool, and when he turned the boat round to come home he stopped the engine, and we just drifted with the current. It was then I first heard the whispering: the bird calls, the fish plopping, the other tiny sounds you'd never hear in broad day. That evening my husband and I were truly joined in spirit.'

A few yards farther on they stopped again to look at the river. They were opposite the men's quarters, and could gaze up the mile-long reach to the mailbox bend. The sun was westering, and its rays coloured the surface with pure gold. The overhanging branches of the twin lines of gums were painted with iridescent greens, and their shadows on the water were black.

The river itself was silent. The late afternoon was drowsily preparing itself for the coming night: roosters crowing, sheep bleating, the voices of men, crows in commotion, an engine softly generating electricity. The sunlight this late winter evening was not unbearable to meet with the eyes, and, since crows always interested Bony with their language, he sought to determine where they were and what they were saying.

A hundred yards above the entry to the shallow billabong separating the river bank from the house garden crows stood on the bank, and others flew about. Settled upon the sheet of gold a foot or so from the bank were two crows, and, because a crow cannot walk on water, they instantly became of interest.

'If you will excuse me, I'd like to see what those birds are excited about,' Bony said. 'Crows are not likeable birds, but they see everything, say everything, know everything.'

'I'll come with you,' said Mrs Cosgrove, dropping her hands from shielding her eyes. 'Have you heard the story of what father crow advised his son? No? Well, father crow said to his son, "If you see a boy, don't fly too near him; and if you see him picking up a stone, fly away fast." The son said, "I'll remember that, father. But what do I do if the boy puts his hand in a pocket?" '

'Unnecessary to try teaching grandmother to suck eggs,' Bony observed, chuckling. They left the levee near the pumping-plant, crossed the billabong to escape the deep-sided entrance, and so came to the bank proper a few yards from the crows, which whirled upwards yelling their protest.

The counter current against the bank held the crows' platform almost motionless. It was lying face downward, only the back of the head and the buttocks showing above the surface. Mrs Cosgrove stifled an exclamation of horror, and Bony felt a swift-rising coldness at the back of his neck.

As the thought had flashed into Bony's mind that the crows probably were attracted by a dead sheep, but might also be attracted by a human body, the shock of the discovery was not instantaneous. Besides, the sun was shining in a flawless sky.

'Please have several men come with ropes and things to get it up,' he said, his voice so calm that it did not betray his emotion. He was conscious of Mrs Cosgrove hastening away while he looked for a forked stick. Finding one, he broke off one branch of it to make a hook, and began the descent to the body.

The exceedingly steep slope was bare of herbage or rock on which to obtain a secure footing and, although dry, it was not reliable because of its pebble-like surface. Bony went downward sideways, and on reaching the water dug with a heel to create a narrow ledge for his feet. Then with the stick he was able to draw the body to the bank and hold it there.

The discovery and the situation of the body were not entirely coincidental. Every experienced bushman can detect the moods of a crow and is familiar with its habits, and any observant person would have noticed the slow but reverse current against the bank. Crouched there, clinging with heels dug into the slope – for to slip would mean not only immersion but great difficulty in crawling from the water with wet hands and clothes – Bony could be pardoned for feeling intensely gratified, if not triumphant. To him it seemed an hour before he heard voices and, looking up, saw the arrival of several men with the overseer. One said, 'Crikey! It's Lush all right.'

'Hold to it, Inspector,' Vickory urged. 'We'll get a rope down to you.'

The end of a rope was fastened about the trunk of a tree, and the free end whirled down to Bony, who with his disengaged hand was able to wind it about his waist. Another rope was so arranged, and the overseer came down by it to join him.

'I'll fix this to it and we can drag it up,' he said, and was stopped.

'Yes, secure the body, but we mustn't drag it up the bank to be further injured. Have someone fetch a wide board or a sheet of iron. Have a rope attached to that. Then we manoeuvre the body to rest on the board or sheet and so bring it up.'

'Good. I see the idea,' said Vickory, and shouted orders.

Two men departed for the sled; others were arriving. The overseer secured the body, and Bony, who was beginning to suffer from cramp, pulled himself up by his rope.

'Is it Lush, Inspector?' asked Ray Cosgrove.

'It would be astonishing were it not,' replied Bony, and flexed his legs to be rid of the stiffness. 'Anyway, the body will have to be put into a shed until a post-mortem can be made. Will you see to that?'

'Of course. Another trip for Leveska, who will roar and scream.'

A man brought a sheet of roofing iron with holes punched at one end to take the rope, and this was lowered to Vickory. He pushed the sheet under the body, and on it the body was drawn up the bank. An old woolsack was placed over it, and, on sticks, sheet and body were conveyed to the carpenter's shop.

Men gathered about outside, including the gang MacCurdle had working in the woolshed. The bearers were told to leave the shed, and then Bony called for a volunteer with a strong stomach. Surprisingly, it was little Jacko who stepped forward, saying he had once been an undertaker's assistant.

He was asked to turn the body on its back, and Bony waited for Ray Cosgrove to identify it.

'It's Lush,' he said, and stumbled out into the last rays of the sun. Bony, whose fear of the dead had always been with him, wanted to rush out after him, but, controlling himself, asked Jacko to remove the clothes. He was forced to turn and stare through the window until the little man said the task was finished.

'Inspector,' Jacko presently called. 'Come and take a decko at this.' Bony knelt opposite him. 'There's a hole in his head, just above the left eyebrow. Could be Bill Lush was shot.'

Chapter Sixteen

Bony Gains Co-operation

The face beyond the corpse was distinctly triangular, tapering sharply from the broad forehead surmounted by thick dark hair to the pointed chin. The eyes were set wide apart. They were hazel in colour, and now bright and excited.

'When I seen him floatin' face down I knew he hadn't been drowned,' said Jacko. 'Drowned people always rise face up. This bloke's got a bullet in him, unless it came out at the back. Wa'da you know?' It was the blue eyes which broke the clash with the hazel eyes. 'Been in the water days, by the look of him. Yabbies been at him, too. No blood, but the hole's here. You can see.'

Bony sensed that the little man had seen the fear in his eyes and even now felt the fear in him. He called to his aid his constant ally, pride, and gazed upon the face of the dead. Jacko placed the tip of a finger on the dead man's forehead. When he withdrew the finger it was obvious that he had performed no great feat of deduction, for the rounded edge of the flesh was torn and lacerated by the yabbies. Bony pressed upon the area with a finger and could feel the circular hole in the frontal bone.

'Any damage denoting exit of bullet?'

Jacko shook his head.

'Can you hold a clothes-peg by the tip of your tongue?' he asked, hoping his voice contained no tremor.

Jacko emitted a sound between a snigger and a chuckle.

'Try me, Inspector. I've had my tongue so loaded with pegs it nearly fell down to me knees. You want me to keep quiet about this?'

'For a few days. Think you could oblige?'

'I'm the most obligin' bloke on the river.'

'Good! Cover it, and let's get out.'

The men had gone, leaving Vickory and Ray Cosgrove to await the outcome of Jacko's administrations. Bony hurried to the shower house as Jacko asked for carbolic, and a couple of plugs of tobacco to go along with. Half an hour later Bony was in contact with Superintendent Macey.

'We have taken the body of William Lush from the river, Super,' he reported. 'Been in the water several days. There is sufficient evidence to indicate that Lush was killed by a bullet.'

'Ah!' breathed the distant police chief. 'Something in the story about the doors after all.'

'There might be.'

'You sound like a cautious lawyer, Bony my old pal. It means, of course, a post-mortem, and this will be difficult to arrange right away. Leveska's gone down to Sydney. Looks as though the body will have to be temporarily buried, unless I can persuade another medic to drive down there. Going to take time by road, too. River's getting miles wide.'

'Very well, Super, I'll have the body buried, and

you will obtain the necessary authorization. Clear?'

'Quite! You got far along the track?'

'I've been looking it over, and started Lucas on inquiries. This latest development is of great interest because not expected.'

'What did you have to do with it? I'll bet you had some part in it.' Bony told about the crows on a voyage. 'Yes, trust you to look-see about those birds. You were in luck, though. The body could well have stayed in the middle of the river and been carried miles downstream, and then it might have been years before it was found, if ever. Still, that's how it's always been with you, Bony. Good reasoning, plus luck. With me it had to be reasoning all along with luck looking in as rarely as a pig sipping beer. I hope to hear from you in the morning.'

Bony next contacted Constable Lucas.

'Should have rung you before, Lucas, but in the first place I was absorbed by other matters, and in the second we have just taken Lush from the river.'

'Then that does start something,' said Lucas.

'Further, it appears likely that Lush was shot through the head.'

'O-oh! The doors again!'

'That's what the Super thinks. I'm not betting on doors at the moment. Did you check with the mail driver?'

'I did. He says that after passing the Crossing, up-river as you'll remember, he met no vehicle, but did meet two swagmen he knew only by sight. They were about three miles south of the utility and travellin' north. He described Dead March Harry and Mick the Warder. Said he warned them about the river,

and they seemed surprised the flood was so near. Can
I be curious, Bony?'

'Curious people invariably have my approval.'

'What's to be done with the body?'

Bony related the gist of his conversation with
Macey, and when Lucas again spoke his voice was
enthusiastic.

'We could get Father Savery to do it. We'll want
that bullet for ballistics, won't we? Soon as possible.'

'I am aware of the urgency,' Bony said, a trifle
stiffly. 'I understand the Father is a Catholic priest.'

'Course he is, Inspector,' agreed Lucas in a manner
betraying that Bony's curtness hadn't gone unnoticed.
'But he's a fully qualified physician, too. I learned
this afternoon when warning the homestead about
Lush that he's staying the night at Linley Downs.
Leaving tomorrow for Bourke. He could make it via
Mira.'

'Think he would do the job for us?'

'No harm done by putting it on him. Shall I
try?'

Bony hesitated before saying, 'I will contact the
Super again, and confer with him. I'm out of my
State – not that I have respect for regulations and
procedure. I'll call you back.'

Superintendent Macey said that Father Savery had
often assisted the law, and that, since Mrs Cosgrove
was a Justice of the Peace, certain formalities could
be observed and the body decently interred. He suggested that he himself should contact Father Savery,
and to this Bony naturally agreed. He was at dinner
when the extension to the house phone shrilled, and
Ray Cosgrove returned to say that Macey wished to
speak to him.

'We are to have a noted visitor tomorrow,' he said when again at table, and, as was his habit, kept them waiting until his hostess asked, 'Well, Bony, who is it?'

'Father Savery,' he replied and then, turning to Ray and Mr MacCurdle, smiled meaningly.

'That will be nice,' Mrs Cosgrove said. 'We mustn't forget the wind indicator, Mac — and be ready to drive over to bring him in immediately we hear his plane. Why is he coming, d'you know?'

'To read the service, one might presume,' Bony replied.

'But Lush isn't, or wasn't, a Catholic.'

'Perhaps he is coming to wish us well in our efforts to vanquish the flood.'

'You can be provocative, Bony,' asserted Ray. 'Now, I'm a good deducer and will work it out. Macey calls you. You tell us Father Savery will be coming tomorrow. We have a dead man on the premises. Being both a priest and a doctor, Father Savery could carry out a post-mortem and then bury him.'

'But he wasn't a Catholic,' Mrs Cosgrove persisted.

'Better be buried by Father Savery than with no one reading over him. Lush won't mind.'

'Your levity isn't appropriate, Ray.'

'Sorry, Mother. I'm right, aren't I, Bony?'

'You are correct,' admitted Bony. 'I admire your perspicacity. It happens that Doctor Leveska is away in Sydney, and thus not available.'

'Wouldn't come, anyway. Leveska attends only desperately ill people.'

Later in the evening Bony begged to be excused as he wished to telephone Constable Lucas from the office. Having informed him of what Superintendent

Macey had done relative to Father Savery, he asked the constable to persuade the flying priest to call first at White Bend.

'I'd like you to fire six shots from that thirty-two, and six from the forty-four. You know, into a blanket hung on a line, or into deep sand. I'd like to have these bullets taken by the Father to Macey, together with the bullet I'm hoping he finds in Lush.'

'I'll talk to Father Savery right away. He'll agree to land here as the strip's in fair condition. The bullet specimens I'll have ready for him. What about the rifles?'

'Keep them in a safe place. Good night.'

When MacCurdle came to the office he found Bony in the private room.

'Come in, Mac, and pay me my shilling,' said Bony.

'You must have worked fast. Coming back with the boss along the levee, I guess.'

'She is imaginative, and Australia has done a lot for her. Sit and smoke. I'd like to gossip for a little while. What kind of man was her husband?'

'Like a playful pup,' replied the manager, 'I didn't meet him until after the war. He was in England when it started, and he joined the R.A.F. His father died in 'forty-three, and through Dalgety's I was sent here to run the place. Mrs Cosgrove senior was also dead. When John Cosgrove came home with his wife and baby Raymond, I was asked to continue. In 'fifty-three John Cosgrove died of cancer, and I lost a good friend.'

'How did you get along with Mrs Cosgrove?'

'At first badly. She was difficult, as you may imagine. I found myself managing her as well as the property. Then we lost the best part of it under

Closer Settlement. Has a rough edge to her tongue, but we get along all right.'

'And the son, Raymond?' pressed Bony.

'Nice enough young chap,' MacCurdle replied. 'Did no good at school, though. Four years down at Wesley. Mrs Cosgrove had plans for him, but in the end she had to give up and let him come home, He's coming to be a good sheep man, however. He was inclined to be uppish for a while, but that was smoothed out.'

'I understand the Cosgroves were friendly with the Maddens. Can you support that?'

MacCurdle hesitated, applying a match to his pipe before saying:

'I can in part. John Cosgrove was very friendly with Madden and his wife. Mrs Cosgrove was always a bit stand-offish.'

'Any reason?'

'Well, you know how it goes, Bony. In Australia a man is placed in the chook order on the job he has and the money he has. In the Old Country he's placed by what his grandfather was, and his father. Jeff Madden was a dam-sinker before he was granted his land under the Closer Settlement. He did well, but once a dam-sinker always a dam-sinker, if you know what I mean.'

'Yes, I do. In confidence, Mac, do you know that young Ray and Jill are very much in love, and that they are afraid of bringing it into the open?'

The manager smiled broadly. 'One day we omitted to send an important letter, and I took it to the box, Ray having already left with the bag. I caught them kissing behind a near-by tree. I think everyone knows, bar Mrs Cosgrove.'

136

'Her reaction would be hostile, you think, also?'

'I feel sure it would. Ray confided in me and I advised him to wait a while.'

'You say everyone. What of Lush?'

'That I don't know. I was referring to people here.'

'I am interested professionally, Mac. Tell me, how does Ray spend his evenings?'

'Reads a bit, I think. Then there's the radio. Spends an hour or so playing cards with the Vickorys . . .'

'Pardon my persistence. Did he often go acourting at night?'

'I expect so.' MacCurdle's eyes twinkled. 'I know I would have done at his age, and having his opportunities.'

MacCurdle saw the blue eyes harden.

'Try to be more explicit.'

'I do recall one night when Ray was wanted by his mother. It was about legal papers. Ray wasn't on hand, and I slipped across to Vickory, and he wasn't there, and he wasn't with the men, as sometimes he might be. He had some explaining to do the next day, and got out of it by saying he'd gone fishing. He admitted to me he'd gone to court Jill Madden as that night Lush was in town.'

Chapter Seventeen

The Flying Priest

The next morning breakfast was advanced by half
an hour, and at seven o'clock heavy engines disturbed
the cold morning and men began work on the levee.
The river had risen five feet, the rise estimated by
MacCurdle at six inches per hour, and the morning
was less golden.

Bony visited the men's cook, a man both solid and
stolid, with no hair, gimlet black eyes and a pale complexion. In the outback he was an oddity, and he
actually spoke with the accent that radio and film
actors habitually use when portraying the common
working man – an accent that originally came from
the inner slums of Sydney and Melbourne, where the
cockney accent once was prevalent.

'Mornin', Inspector.'

'Good morning. You are headed for a lot of
work.'

'Yers. Ten extra to deal with. And you got a corpse
on your 'ands. Me offsider was telling us Lush ain't
very 'andsome these dies. He never was, but a bit
worse than usual.'

'Not having met him when he was alive, I am unable to criticize his present appearance,' Bony said

with an inward shudder, and from somewhere in the vicinity of his carpet slippers the cook produced a chuckle.

Bony found Jacko splitting wood for the baking ovens.

'Mornin', Inspector. How's things?'

'Average, Jacko, average. Think the cook could spare you for an hour or so later in the morning? Father Savery is headed this way and may want assistance.'

'O.K. by me,' said Jacko, adding softly, 'Is he goin' to dig out that bullet?'

'If it's there. And then the body will have to be buried. Did you know Lush well enough to sign a statement of identity?'

'Know him! He was the greatest bastard on the river. Sign for him! Too right, I'll sign and sing a song of joy when doing it.'

'Then I'll send for you when Father Savery needs you.'

Returning to the house, Bony sought Mrs Cosgrove and asked would she please accompany him to the office. They observed MacCurdle and Ray departing with a theodolite, and Bony invited Mrs Cosgrove to sit in the inner or private room.

'Being aware of what the outcome of the post-mortem will be, I shall need to call on your services as a Justice,' he said. 'It will be necessary for you to sign affidavits covering identity, and also statements concerning the operation of the post-mortem, as the body will have to be interred here. I could not ask Father Savery to convey it to Bourke, since it will not be necessary. He is being very co-operative as it is.'

'Anything you wish, Bony. It has to be done, un-pleasant though it may be. And then we can give our attention to the flood.' Mrs Cosgrove pursed her lips; the phrase 'a well-preserved woman' suited her this morning; she was without make-up, and dressed for business.

'The result of the post-mortem will not be what you are thinking, and I want to take you into my confidence because the case has become most serious. You see, Lush wasn't drowned: he was shot.'

'Oh! That is bad.' Mrs Cosgrove regarded Bony intently. 'By Jill? That night she sat up waiting for Lush?'

'We shall not know for some days.'

'She told me straight out that if Lush had broken into the house she would have shot him. I for one would not blame her. The circumstances were terrible for her.'

'My opinion will be influenced by what Father Savery discovers. We must keep our minds open. Quite apart from the case, I find myself liking Jill. What is your feeling?'

'Quite a nice young woman,' answered Mrs Cosgrove. 'The school gave her tone and manners. Of course, this is the first occasion I've met her socially, as it were. I agree we must keep open minds, and I shall continue to be Christian in my attitude.'

'I am sure you will. We were talking yesterday, and I rather think she would be happier if you could find her something to do in this flood crisis -- after the result of the post-mortem is known.'

'Yes, I think that would be wise. All right, I'll find something to occupy her. You don't know when Father Savery will arrive?'

'Not precisely. Some time this morning. The indicator in position?'

'Yes. I thought you and I could run out to meet him. He'll let us know when he arrives. He's a wonderful man.'

Father Savery let them know of his arrival by flying low along the straight river reach, roaring upwards over the men's quarters and circling the big house without spinning his wheels on the roof. Mrs Cosgrove drove the car the half-mile to the landing-strip, and they were in time for Bony to help anchor the machine against the wind.

Father Savery was a very large man padded by energetic muscles rather than fat. His face was large, too, and topped by stiff brown hair which increased his six feet by at least three inches. His voice was soft and distinctly English, and when he was introduced to Bony his hazel eyes became the centre of radiating wrinkles.

'I have a package for you from Constable Lucas. Remind me of it. I have, too, a message from Super-intendent Macey to the effect that you are ordered to return to your headquarters in Brisbane at once, leaving here with me today.'

'How kind of Superintendent Macey to convey the order, Father, and how kind of you to transmit it! So much time in the past has been ill spent with such trivialities. I've no doubt that further time will be wasted in the future.'

'Ha! A rebel! A confounded non-conformist. I've been told a great deal of you. Some say you won't even conform with non-conformity. What is your opinion of him, Betsy Cosgrove?'

'He won't give me time enough to form an opinion,'

Mrs Cosgrove replied, and braked the car to a stop outside the office. 'Now come along, both of you, and we'll have morning tea on the veranda.'

Father Savery appeared quite uninterested in the cause of his visit, for he talked about Mrs Cosgrove's neighbours at homesteads upward of a hundred miles away. With Jill Madden present, Bony considered it most diplomatic of him. Afterwards Bony escorted the priest to the office and there told him of the suspected wound in the dead man's head.

'If the bullet is still in the body we shall need it for ballistics, Father.'

'That won't be difficult, Inspector. Macey hinted that the death wasn't accidental. You have, of course, had the body identified as that of William Lush. An ill-disposed man. His wife, God rest her, was a homely, gentle woman. Well, shall we get to him?'

'It's on the floor of the carpenter's shop. You'll want it on the bench, I presume. I'll call for an undertaker's assistant. Excuse me for a minute.'

Bony drove to the men's kitchen and collected the small man who, when he eventually stood beside the priest, was dwarfed.

Father Savery boomed out, 'I know you, Jacko. What happened to that daughter of yours?'

'Got married to a butcher, your reverence. Down at Mildura. Doing well. Got another kid and all.'

'Glad to hear it. Glad she didn't turn out like her worthless father. You are still a vagrant, I suppose.'

'Who, me, Father! I'm workin'.'

'Excellent! Keep on.'

Conducted to the shop, Father Savery supervised the placing of the body on the carpenter's bench. Bony stood at the window, refusing to look at the operation.

Jacko, however, took a deep interest in it. Bony heard the following chit-chat.

'That's where the bastard got it, Father. Sorry, your reverence. Just there, the bullet went in. Bet a quid on it.'

'Humph! Get out of the light. Must be shot to death. Don't look drowned.'

'Came up arse first,' asserted Jacko. 'Drowned men come up stomach first.'

'Interesting, Jacko, but mere theory. No corresponding wound, so it should be inside the skull. Bullets become erratic after entry. Didn't know I was a military surgeon in the last war, did you?'

'Was you, Father? Crikey!'

'So you see, experience in tracing bullets will be of value this morning. Hold the head, so. Keep it steady.'

'Reminds me,' said Jacko. 'Me and the boss had to collect a body one day. We arrives with the basket. The bloke's lying on the bed pretty comfortable like, and just then the telephone in the hall goes off and the boss answers it as there's no one around. Then the boss rushes back yelling, "Hop it, Jacko! We're in the wrong house!"'

'You're not looking at what you should be doing,' said the priest. 'Keep your eyes on the job.'

'I thought I was good, Father. Now I'm not feeling so bright.'

'Keep your mind on the work, not your stomach. Now, where do we find the bullet? There was one feller I investigated for a bullet. Point of entry was below the left ear, and the point of exit was between the second and third rib on the left side. Ha, this could be it. No, hold to it. The feller would have been upset if he'd woken up and found himself in a basket. Reminds me— Ha! Here it is, Jacko. A nice shapely little thing fired from a ·32 calibre gun. Astonishing! It must have orbited inside the skull. Push the stuff into the bucket, and we'll take a look or two at the lungs.'

'I'd sooner do the embalming, Father.'

'No preferences. Get along with it.'

'That's funny,' observed Jacko a moment or two later. 'Looks like sheep's lungs to me. How's she coming?'

'No water there. Dead on immersion.'

'Wish I'd been educated. Ten to one on that emershion word.'

'Now we'll clean up, Jacko. And thanks for your help.'

'All right by me, Father. I'll empty this lot, and be right back.' Bony would not have turned for a hundred pounds.

Father Savery chuckled, saying, 'We'll be respectable again in a minute, Inspector. Every man to his trade. I'll have friend Jacko wash the bullet.'

'Can you say whether the bullet was fired at close range?' Bony asked.

'No, I cannot. As I mentioned, the course of such a projectile is always erratic after entry. Being ignorant of the muzzle velocity I could not even offer a guess. Anyway, there's no evidence of burning, but that amounts to nothing since the yabbies attacked the wound.'

Jacko returned to say:

'Crikey! You got him lookin' pretty, Father. All ready for the box. If there's one handy. For me, I'd bulldoze him into the levee. The bas—'

'That'll do, Jacko,' Father Savery told him, sternly.

'The man's life is no longer our affair, but we must respect the Almighty's creation. Now wash the gloves after we place the body in this woolsack, and then remove the iron sheet outside and swill that down. I shall ask Mrs Cosgrove to make you a present of half a pound of tobacco.'

Bony stepped outside and breathed deeply. Ten minutes later he was joined by the priest.

'There was a fellow in a house who discharged a bullet from a ·32 calibre rifle,' Bony said. 'The bullet passed through the plaster ceiling and then through the iron roof above it. If the man who slew Lush was standing, say, about ten feet from him, would not the bullet have passed right through his head?'

'Hard question, Inspector. Everything depends on angles and curves, and distance from the gun to the point of impact. Is your question important?'

'Until the laboratory determines that the bullet you recovered was or was not fired from the gun Lucas fired this morning, yes. To have that information will take days. I'll parcel this bullet you found in Lush and, with the packet you brought from Lucas, ask you to deliver it to the Superintendent as quickly as possible.'

'You speak in riddles, but I'll do as you ask. You will be returning to Bourke with me?'

'No, Father. I shall not be returning to Bourke until I have completed my investigation. How would you feel to be ordered from church in the middle of your discourse?'

'I might lose my temper.'

'I try not to lose mine, but often I have to make a real effort not to lose my patience.'

'You are refreshing, Inspector. It's been a pleasure

meeting you. Now I'll return and scrub up. A surgeon, yes. But I am not as tough as friend Jacko. He's completely insensitive. And fortunate.'

'Greatly so when on the scales with me, Father. Please come to the office when you can.'

Chapter Eighteen

At the Swagmen's Camp

The ten swagmen taken on by Mrs Cosgrove elected to remain at the shearers' quarters instead of moving to the men's quarters. They were united by the tenuous bond of the track, influenced by the same spiritual power activating the Aborigines. They were much closer to the secret nature of this land than is the average employee on stations, some of whom stay put for years.

When the wind again came coldly from the south-east they were gathered about the open fire between shed and levee, some seated on their heels, others on old cases or kerosene tins. The wind played upon a near-by gum tree. The river had a voice all its own, and the firelight painted red the faces of the only free men in Australia. When Bony drew near they were trying to persuade Jacko to tell them the outcome of the post-mortem.

Jacko had skated close to the truth. With verve he had described Father Savery's manipulation of knife and saw, making awful comparisons between the body of William Lush and those of road-accident victims he had serviced in his former profession. Yet his audience knew he was keeping something back. He was on the verge of desperation when Bony stepped from black night into the ring.

'You can release the news now, Jacko,' he said, and sat on a spare petrol tin. Making a cigarette, he waited for Jacko to talk, and felt the stony silence, and was aware of the hard eyes directed at him. Being a policeman, he was beyond the pale to these men, though they could not be classified as law-breakers; their attitude was inherited from the bad old days.

'I asked Jacko not to broadcast what happened to Lush,' he told them. 'I did this so that Lush's stepdaughter would not learn of it by a roundabout track. Since I've been here I haven't heard one good word for Lush, but I have heard much sympathy expressed for his unfortunate wife. What mystifies me is why Lush wasn't dealt with years ago. Now, Jacko.'

'Well, it was this here,' Jacko began; then, expertly squirting tobacco juice at the large fire, he restrained his relief and continued to tease the men's curiosity. 'The pardray says to me did I think he oughter take a decko at Lush's lungs to make sure he had drowned. I said it would be a good idea, although I was positive Lush hadn't drowned as he'd come up arse first. The Inspector will back me up on that.'

Jacko paused, and Bony nodded agreement.

'It's a well-known fact that a body in water what's been drowned comes up belly first, and, as I've said, Lush came up the other way round.'

'You've said all that before,' asserted Mick the Warder.

'Well, the pardray agreed, and he opened up Lush, and we didn't find a drop of water in him. I could see the pardray looking a bit concerned, like, and I suggested that Lush could've been bumped off by something like a rock he hit when he fell over the cliff.'

'Who was doing the bloody job, you or the Father?' mildly inquired the large man called Wally Watts.

'We was doing it together. I held him and the pardray sliced him,' Jacko compromised. 'Well, then we looked him over, and blow me down if I didn't find a bullet hole in his head. Ain't that right, Inspector?'

'Quite right,' Bony agreed. 'You found the bullet hole.'

'So we mucks him around to see where the bullet come out, and it hasn't come out. Then the pardray says we'll have to take a bit off his crust and look around inside. And there was the bullet, a nice little thirty-two.'

Jacko again paused, this time as though expecting applause. Silence descended upon them, and in the background could be heard the soft gurgling of water and the barking of a distant fox.

'He was shot,' a grizzled elderly man said flatly.

'He was shot. He had a thirty-two in his head,' Jacko assured the company. 'All nicely planted in the old conk. You know, a bloke didn't oughter be surprised, but I was, even though he hadn't come up belly first. He shoulda been shot years ago. That's so, eh, Champion?'

The white-haired, white-moustached man who had previously related William Lush's origin nodded his heavy head.

'That's so, Jacko,' he said. 'Old Bill Lush made his pub pay handsome. Ma Lush worked like ten women, and give away some of what her husband made. She was a grand woman. Never see a man go hungry, and never let him loose on the track after he'd spent his cheque without a full tucker-bag and a half-bottle to get him over the screws. They should have joined hands and strangled the kid at birth. He put both of 'em in their graves and scattered what they had to the four winds.'

'Then he comes down here, marries Mrs Madden, kicks her to death, and gets a bullet in the conk,' concluded Mick the Warder.

'And the police'll arrest the bloke what done it and jail him for ten years,' said a lean man with a squint. 'Ain't that so, Inspector?'

'It's the law. I didn't make it,' Bony said. 'I saw Mrs Lush after she died, and I agree with Champion that he should have died much earlier.'

'There! What did I tell you blokes?' demanded Jacko. 'Where in 'ell would we be if it wasn't for the coppers? You tell me. Why, the big blokes like Wally Watts would rule the flaming roost, and little blokes like me'd be bashed to death for looking sideways.'

'I got no time for 'em. Never did have,' said a solemn man wearing a coat the rents of which the wind was flapping.

'Can't say I have, either, but we gotta have 'em all the same,' argued Jacko.

A very tall man who had been sitting on a case and resting his elbows on his knees straightened and from the pocket of his old green overcoat withdrew a harmonica. The firelight gleamed upon it. He placed it to his lips and produced one note before Mick the Warder reached and took it from him.

'None of that, Harry. We're workin',' he said quietly.

The would-be player made no protest and resumed

his former attitude. Bony recognized him. He was Dead March Harry, shaved and barbered.

'What beats me,' said Champion, 'is how Lush got to be where he was found. I'd have thought he'd have been collected by the first rush of water. Musta been in a hole up-river, likely enough in the hole where his ute was found, but you'd think when the first wave of rubbish tumbled into it he'd have come up. But he don't. He bides a while and then comes up to float, nice and quiet like, downstream.'

'What d'you reckon, Inspector?' asked the large Wally Watts.

'I'm not an expert on bodies in water, drowned or otherwise,' Bony admitted. 'That seems to be Jacko's hobby. The condition of Lush's body certainly proves it had been in water for several days. I think we could bet it was in the hole below the mail-boxes. According to Jacko, Lush didn't drown: he was dead when he fell into the hole or was dropped into it. The body would, I think, sink quickly and finally rest on a log or sodden branch at the bottom.

'The bottom being so far down, when the first and subsequent flood rushes past into and across the hole it wouldn't have been disturbed. When, according to natural law, it rose, the river was feet deep, and the current sweeping round the bend brought it to the straight reach, then brought it across to the opposite side, this side. If you study the surface of the river you'll see that along the edge there are short reverse currents holding against the bank small masses of debris, and one of these reverse currents caught and held the body.'

'Easy when you know how,' a man said to his neighbour.

'You was lucky to walk along the bank and spot him,' commented Champion.

'I didn't spot him. I saw two crows that appeared to be standing on water, and others flying about. As we all know, crows don't walk on water. They will stand on a dead sheep. Those two were standing on the body of Lush.'

'And you put two and two together took a chance what come off,' said Mick the Warder. 'Well, I don't suppose they made you an inspector unless they had to.'

'You could be right,' agreed Bony, laughing. Several others joined in. They were beginning to accept him because he showed none of the officiousness they were accustomed to meet in a policeman. They were aware, too, that education had raised him far above the average; they heard it in his voice, sensed it in his easy manner, for they had all encountered at some time the wealthy station owner in whom there was no condescension, and the minister of religion who had learned to mix without it.

'Now you'll be looking for the bloke who fixed Lush,' Wally Watts said. 'A bullet in him sort of discards the idea that he fell into the hole in the dark.'

'I shall be looking for that man.'

'Think you'll find him?' asked Mick the Warder.

'The flood is going to make the job difficult.'

'Don't like your chances,' said Jacko. 'Crikey! The blokes what's been knocked off along this river! 'Undreds of 'em. They got the Man They Couldn't Drop down at Taylor's Crossing, socked it into him right and left, put him up on the block, and the jury wouldn't slug him. So out he comes, just because they couldn't find the body. Then he tells 'em he done it,

and they can all take a runnin' jump over theirselves
'cos they can't try a man twice. Wonder what 'appened
to him. Anyone know?'

'Yair. He camped with us a coupler months back,'
said the man with the squint. 'Still going strong. She's
a great little river to go disappearin' in. You hear
about that case, Inspector? Away back in 'thirty-nine?'

'Before my time,' replied Bony.

'Well, the Man They Couldn't Drop was skinnin'
a sheep by the river, and two kids come along and
watched him. Then they ran home and told their old
man about it. He grabbed a rifle, and raced down to
where the kids said they seen the sheep being skinned.
He never turned up no more. After a bit his wife and
the kids went to look for him and found the Man
They Couldn't Drop asleep and the sheep's carcass
hanging up under a tree. There's no skin: only the
carcass and chop bones what he had grilled. He's
charged with murder. He says if he had killed the
bloke he'd have done a get. But he was too cunnin'.
Seems that the bloke charged at him, and he took the
gun off him and used the butt. Just slipped the body
into the river.'

'I've always had a lot of time for this river,' said
Champion. 'You got a body and a bullet, Inspector,
but the river will balk you.'

'It could,' said Bony. 'But I shall have to try to
find the man who shot Lush.'

'How will you go about it, Inspector?' Squint-eye
asked.

Smiling disarmingly, Bony explained. 'It is known
that Lush left White Bend at about ten-thirty on the
night of July 19. It's known, too, that when under
the influence he drove exceptionally slowly, and so

153

it's thought that he arrived at the mail-boxes about midnight. No one has come forward to say he saw the abandoned utility before the station mail was taken to the box by young Cosgrove at 11.45 the next morning. That's almost twelve hours after Lush is presumed to have abandoned it because of lack of petrol.

'During the period no vehicle passed either way, as far as the police can ascertain. The ground thereabouts is powdery and the night was windy. I could see no footprints when I went there late the next day, or on succeeding days, and so there's no evidence as yet that Lush was shot at or near those boxes.'

'Perhaps he was shot at his own place,' said Squint-eye.

'As likely there as anywhere else. He might have been shot at this homestead. He might have been shot at the camp of three men known as The Brothers, who were on the far side of the river. Everyone disliked him so much that anyone could have had motive enough to kill him. Because his body was discovered up-river from this homestead it's almost certain he was shot somewhere up-river.

'The question then arises: who could have shot him, taking into account the time period and distance. Mrs Cosgrove could have killed him. So, too, could Jill Madden. Most unlikely, but possible. Any man on Mira could have killed him. The three men called The Brothers could have done so. It's possible that any one of you could have done it.'

Bony looked from one to the other, and paused while he made a cigarette. No one spoke. Then: 'It's my job to find out who removed William Lush from this world. Because I'm paid to do so, I shall do my best. To this there is a side issue I've never been able

to understand. The law says in effect Thou Shalt Not.
When someone says "I shall" he knows well enough
that he's bucking the law. Then what? Well, he
gambles against being caught. When caught, ninety-
nine killers in every hundred moan and groan, and
spit fire at the police. They don't moan when they
lose a quid on a horse, or miss out on a lottery prize
by one digit. The average man's a pretty good sportsman, so why can't he be equally sporting if he gambles
with the law and loses out?'

'What about the police telling lies, swearing a man's
life away?' asked a man who had not spoken before.

'It doesn't stop with the police. The feller you call
the Man They Couldn't Drop was discharged by a
jury at court. Afterwards he admitted he had killed
the sheep owner. I'd say he was a good sportsman, a
keen gambler. Anyway, it's the way I look at it. I
gamble on finding who killed Lush; then let the man
who shot him gamble that I don't. There's nothing
personal about it on my side. So why should he be
personal about it? He laid the odds.'

'Fair enough,' Jacko said, once more squirting
tobacco juice. 'Big bloke bashes a little bloke, and he
starts a gamble that a bigger bloke don't bash 'im. If
he loses he's got no right to moan.'

'And further to this case we are discussing,' Bony
went on, 'you may accept it from me that I'll go all
out to find out who killed Lush, and at the same time
I shall be hoping he'll win the gamble, Lush was a
type who should be shot.'

'You know, you're a funny man,' said the solemn
man in the torn coat. 'I wouldn't be surprised—'

He was stopped by the abrupt movement of Dead
March Harry. Harry stood and stared over the fire at

155

the invisible river, and from his mouth issued the first 'Bomb!' He turned slowly about and took a step towards the shed and vented another 'Bomb!'

Mick the Warder got up and clutched him by the arm, saying, 'You come out of it, Harry. We're workin', and there's no time for that.'

'I'm dead! I'm dead!' Harry repeated, and strode away with measured tread, the rotund Mick clinging to his arm; and thus they passed from the view of the men about the fire.

'I shall need to question all of you tomorrow,' Bony told them. 'I shall need to know where each of you was on the night of July 18–19 and the following morning until noon. You can give your statements in station time.'

Chapter Nineteen

The 'Rine' Came Down

Bony woke to hear rain on the iron roof. In the breakfast-room he met a very disturbed Mr MacCurdle,
and an equally disturbed Raymond Cosgrove.

'Out of the blue,' declared the manager. 'Not predicted by the weather people. It began shortly after
four this morning.'

'Just measured it. Eighty-three points so far, and
no sign of stopping,' added Ray. 'Wonderful fall at
a very good time.'

'Provided the run-off doesn't coincide with the
crest of the flood. Get the two together, and we could
be in trouble.'

'Stop the men working?' asked Bony, and they
told him the rain would only slow the work at the
levee.

Outside he thought it was a wonderful morning.
It hadn't rained for several months; the earth was
sopping up the precious moisture and giving in return the aromatic scents which only semi-arid land
can produce. When an hour had passed he contacted
Superintendent Macey.

'Yes, we sent the samples down to Ballistics,' Macey
told him. 'Should have their report some time this

afternoon. Looks like the bullet through the door killed Lush, doesn't it?'

'It could be so,' said Bony cautiously. 'I'll be waiting for that report, Super. Raining up your way?'

'Hard. Over an inch already. Everyone's dancing with joy. Making Mira a bit mucky, I suppose. Father Savery would have been bogged today. What d'you think of him?'

'Born to this outback,' answered Bony. 'I've met a lot of good churchmen, but only one like Father Savery, and he was a Bush Brother. I hope you thanked him properly.'

'Be sure on that point, Bony. He told us he had fine help from a mortician's assistant.'

'Little man called Jacko.'

'He mentioned the name. No record of him. The yarn about being in the wrong house was a funny one. Jacko's somewhat of a character. You're lucky. All we get are drunks.'

'Ah! But I train the characters, Super. Bring them out with kindness. I've a list of names I'd like checked with records. Will you note them, please?' Bony read his list of ten, and Macey said he would have them checked and ring back. He was on the phone again in thirty minutes.

'About your characters, Bony. Ready?'

Bony wrote:

Jacko. Clean.
Dead March Harry. Clean.
Mick the Warder. Clean.
Champion. Six months for stealing a horse.
Wally Watts. Clean.

Bill, Ned and Silas, known as The Brothers.
Bill: Clean. Ned: Drunk and disorderly. Silas:
Theft.
Bosun Dean. Clean.
The Paroo Bikeman. Assault and battery.

Of the six men employed under overseer Vickory,
five had been charged on the D. and D. offence at
White Bend.

'Got all that?' asked the Superintendent. 'Good!
Then there's Master Ray. Drunk in charge of a motor
vehicle here in Bourke: D. and D. at White Bend.
That's as much as we have. The Paroo Bikeman's
your worst character, and after him come The
Brothers, right name Wishart. Why didn't you return with Father Savery yesterday?'

'I wouldn't fly with him for promotion to Chief
Commissioner,' said Bony. 'And now I cannot relin-
quish the assignment. Rain makes the tracks too
boggy. And I did want to go home.'

'That's what you're saying, my Artful Dodger. Bye-
bye.'

Bony borrowed MacCurdle's overcoat and
umbrella and went off for a stroll along the levee.
The rain was steady and showed no sign of ceasing.
The river was within six feet of the top of the bank
where they had retrieved the body; within hours it
would be pouring into the billabong behind the
house garden. A rainfall of three to four inches would
present trouble to Mira.

He found Jacko peeling potatoes on the back
veranda of the men's kitchen, and sat with him to
roll a cigarette.

'Every drop a quid to the squatter and a penny to

the stockman,' quoted the 'little bloke'. 'How you doing, Inspector?'

'You might be able to help me do a little better,' Bony said. 'For instance, where were you on the morning of July 19?'

'That was when Lush sort of disappeared. I was camped that night at the Mackham Downs wool-shed. The next day, that's the day you want, Inspector, I was still camped there, 'cos I didn't leave till the following day.'

'Where is this station?'

'Eighteen miles south of White Bend on this side of the river.'

'And you came up here on this side of the river?'

'Yes. I didn't even cross at White Bend. I had no dough.'

'Clears you, it appears. Tell me, Jacko, who of the men at the camp fire last night is the Paroo Bike-man?'

'Now look here, Inspector, I don't want to cross anyone up.'

'I wouldn't want you to. You could tell me who is the man called the Bikeman, surely?'

'All right, but don't tell him I told you. He's a nasty bit of work. He was sittin' next to Champion. Never said a word all through. Feller with a small mouth and black moustache.'

'Could you bring yourself to tell me why that elderly man is called Champion?'

'Too right!' replied Jacko, and smiled. 'He was working out on Yandama, up in the Corner, when he won a pretty good prize in a lottery. So he and three more pulled out and headed for Milparinka. He says to the three blokes with him he'd give a hundred quid to the bloke who could drink more pints of beer than him, taking 'em one a minute. He'd pay for the beer.

'So they all get set, and the publican gets set, too. One pint per minute, with the yardman follerin' the clock. Well, off they goes, and mind you, none of 'em's had a beer for months. No trainin' and no cheatin', see.

'The first bloke give up after the fifth pint. The next one couldn't go after his eighth. That left one with Champion, and they ran neck and neck to the eleventh pint, when the last bloke shut his eyes and fell over on the floor. The yarn goes that Champion went on to down his twenty-first pint in the twenty-one minutes, and that he was disqualified by the yardman for taking more'n a minute to down his twenty-second. It made him sort of lose interest in beer, and he called for whisky – what the publican refused on account of not wanting a corpse on his 'ands.'

'And that's as true as I'm standing here,' said the cook from his kitchen door. 'Course, Champion was twenty years younger than now. He was a champion shearer, too, but sheep don't have anything to do with him winning the beer championship. Nice rine, ain't it, Inspector?'

'Very,' agreed Bony. 'How long have you been cooking here?'

'Fourteen months. 'Bout time I took a spell and tried to beat Champion on the beer. Only I don't drink beer. Gin's me tonic. And besides, I'm aiming to take a trip over to New Zealand. Excuse me! The . brownie!'

Bony followed the cook into the spacious kitchen-dining-room, where he sat at the range end of the long table and waited for the cook to attend to his cake in the oven.

'The three men called The Brothers,' he began when the cook sat opposite and drew on a cigarette. 'How long were they camped across the river?'

'Oh, three-four weeks.'

'Did they come often for a handout?'

'One of 'em would come over twice a week, I suppose. They had dough, though, because they bought tucker off'n the store.' The cook regarded Bony steadily. 'Seems that Lush was knocked,' he said. 'The men were still talking about it at breakfast.'

'Good talking point,' Bony said, and rose to leave. 'By the noise they must be working in the rain.'

'Some of 'em are at bonus rates. The machines are makin' the row. The missus is gettin' anxious, like, now this rine's on.'

Bony went on to the shearing-shed, where he found Mick the Warder reading a paper.

'Day, Inspector!'

'Good day, Mick. Where's Harry?'

'In his bunk. He had a bad night. Talking about bodies and things upset him. Gets that way, as you know.'

'D'you know how he came to be like that?'

'Yes. He got tossed off a horse at a rodeo. Landed on his head. He sort of come round all right and seemed all right for six months. Then he took to the track, and I'm camped one night when I hear him on the march, and he stood over me to tell me he was dead. I sort of took pity on him, and we been travellin' ever since.'

'And look after him that he comes to no hurt. Why

did you get out from the prison service? Any reason
I shouldn't know?'

'No. I was broke up when the wife and son was
both killed in a road accident. That's all. When I
pulled out I came up here, and I'm glad I did.'

'The subject of relations between men and the
police came up last night, Mick. What was the reaction you met with from the swagmen?'

'The no-hopers, Inspector!' The rotund man
grinned. 'No trouble at all, after a bit, and after I
dealt with a couple lookin' for fight. They think a
lot of poor Harry, and I suppose they think something of me, too.'

'They should. Where were you two when Lush is
thought to have been shot?'

'Murrimundi. In an old hut at the wool-scour.
About a couple of mile up-river from the homestead.'

'Good! Tell me, where were you making for that
day I met you in Madman's Bend?'

'Well, we did think of camping and doing a spot
of fishing in the hole under the mail-boxes,' replied
Mick the Warder. 'Then we reckoned we'd call in
at Mrs Madden's as Harry always got on well with
her. You know, Harry used to work now and then
for Madden. In fact, we both took jobs at times from
Madden.'

'How did you get on with Lush?' Bony asked,
maintaining an easy front.

'Didn't get on ever. No one did. But Mrs Madden
could have her way sometimes.'

'You say, Mick, that you were camped at Murrimundi wool-scour. Didn't you see Lush pass on his
way down to White Bend?'

'Couldn't have. The old scour's a mile off the road

in a bend. No, we had no idea about Lush being missing until we got here after seeing you.' Mick the Warder grinned humourlessly. 'You're going to be unpopular if you nail the man who murdered Lush.'

'It would seem so, since everyone disliked him intensely.' Bony stood to go. 'You know, if I lost my people, I, too, would take to the track. See you again, Mick.'

A quarter-mile beyond the shearing-shed the levee turned away from the river and took a wide sweep to enclose the entire homestead. The 'dozer was working out there beyond sight, and Bony guessed that all the men were there with it and the loader. There being no wind, the rain fell straight, a steady watering-can fall that created puddles and inexorably enlarged them; its soft pattering on them and on the leaves of the gum tree by the swagmen's fire was the note that kept vividly in Bony's mind the mateship of one man with another, the bond uniting a strong man with one afflicted.

There being no sun, he had to wait till the office clock informed him of the time, and he was sitting in the manager's room when MacCurdle and Ray Cosgrove returned from their work with the theodolite.

'A rare morning, Bony, and we need a drink,' the manager said breezily. 'D'you think you could be persuaded?'

'I do think,' replied Bony, and Ray said he would go in for a bottle of beer.

MacCurdle brought a bottle of whisky from a cupboard, put it on the table, and went out for water. Bony idly noted that the bottle was sealed, and that it was wrapped in the usual tissue paper. The manager came back with the water jug, and ripped away the tissue, nailed off the seal, drew the cork, and poured as though his life depended on it. Bony helped himself to a light portion, and over the glasses both smiled. There was nothing remarkable about this, but it set a fly buzzing against the window of Bony's memory.

'The rain's steady, and the river's rising faster because of the local run-off, Bony. The levee sunders and only the house and this office will stand above water. You'll probably be with us a long, long time. Still, there's nine more bottles in my private cupboard. Help yourself when you want.'

Ray came in with his bottle of beer, filled his glass twice, rolled a cigarette, dangled a leg over the arm of a chair.

'Mum's having a wonderful time,' he said. Bony raised his brows. 'Out there in the rain with the men. Directing them, sooling them on, and the rest. They're going on strike if she isn't a bit more casual. Should have known by now that the Australian won't take orders from a woman. She'll learn.'

'Never,' said MacCurdle firmly.

'If they down tools we'd better learn to swim.'

'Can't you swim? I thought every boy was taught to swim,' commented Bony.

'I mean long distance. You know, about twenty miles.'

The telephone rang, and the manager went out to take the call. It was for Bony. Macey spoke.

'The ballistics report's just come to hand. The doors are out. The bullet in Lush wasn't fired from the rifle belonging to the Maddens.'

Chapter Twenty

'Just Pottering About'

'Ah! There you are! I've been looking for you, Jill.'

'Have you, Inspector?' The girl was seated at a sewing-machine, and her dark eyes searched his face.

He sat down and said, 'Good news, Jill. The bullet you fired through the back door didn't kill Lush. The laboratory fellers have proved it. Unless you had another thirty-two rifle, or a pistol I didn't find.'

'There were only the thirty-two and the forty-four, Inspector.'

'Then the little, tiny, tenuous, make-believe shadow is lifted from you. I could not be confident about you till now, Jill, and I am truly happy. I left Ray with Mac, and I'll leave you to tell him, and we can all forget about that night of tension. By the way, can you remember a man calling for tucker known as the Paroo Bikeman?'

'Yes, I can. I saw him once. Nasty eyes. Dad said he always travelled light, and could ride a hundred miles a day over any kind of track. He's been known to be in Bourke one week, and down at Mildura the next. Lush was terrified of him. Would always have Mother see to his handout.'

'When was the last time he called for a handout?'

'A week or ten days before Lush left the utility. I can't be exact. I was out when he called, and Mother just mentioned it.'

'Did she tell you which way he was travelling?'

Jill shook her head, and Bony persisted.

'The three men who were camped down here opposite the shearing-shed who are called The Brothers — did they come for a handout lately?'

'No. I know who you mean. They haven't come to us for a long time. I remember Dad saying they were the greatest loafers in the outback.'

'Thanks, Jill. If you think of anything unusual happening just before Lush tried to smash down the door, please tell me. Or of anyone calling at the house.'

Cosgrove was informed that Jill wanted to speak to him, and to the manager Bony directed questions concerning the Paroo Bikeman and the others. Mac-Curdle had little information on the no-hopers, save that he sold them tobacco and tinned food at odd times, and Bony was aware that he would not come in contact with them so much as would the men's cook. He knew that The Brothers had been camped for several weeks on the far bank because they had bought tobacco from his store.

Lunch that day was a quiet affair, Mrs Cosgrove saying little and betraying annoyance over what Bony surmised was her failure to get from the men the work she thought they should have done despite the discomforts caused by the weather. Once he caught Ray impishly winking at Jill, and once he found MacCurdle giving Ray a warning glance.

After lunch Bony went to his room and lay on the bed, and there fought to make his mind disgorge an item it had registered. He fell asleep during the battle, and on waking found that it was after four o'clock. It was still raining. Again in the office, he contacted Constable Lucas.

'Ballistics report that the bullet which killed Lush wasn't fired from the rifle you have,' Bony said, and Lucas's voice told him that the policeman was glad to hear it. 'I'm going to give you the names of ten men, all come in off the track and now working here. Jot them down.' Lucas recorded the names. 'We know where The Brothers were camped that vital night and morning. Jacko says he was camped at Markham Downs. Harry and Mick the Warder were camped at the old wool-scour at Murrimundi. Will you check as closely as you can?'

'Will do. What about the others?'

'Trace their movements at that period, and meanwhile I'll question them. There could have been others in the vicinity, on the way up- or down-river.'

'I'll do my best, Bony. How's the flood with you?'

'They're worried that the run-off from the rain will raise the level to make conditions dangerous. Been working all day despite the rain. I haven't manned a shovel yet.'

'You will,' predicted the policeman. 'It's going to cut White Bend off, too, if this rain continues. The weather men who didn't predict it now predict it won't last overnight.'

Having hung up, Bony relaxed in the easy chair and rolled a cigarette. In front of him was the wastepaper basket, and the latest contribution in it was the wrapping from MacCurdle's whisky bottle. There again came that nagging sense of frustration, and two seconds after it began the mind surrendered. He remembered the small piece of tissue paper he had found in the heart of Madman's Bend, found and discarded, contemptuously tossed aside as something captured by the wind.

There was a wall mirror, and he stood before it and glowered at his reflection. From the mirror there came to him the words he spoke softly:

'Am I growing old and tired? That piece of paper could have been part of a bottle wrapper. Supposition. Easy deduction. It isn't like me to forget about it. Yes, you are growing old. You are coming to be mentally limited, able to think only of one subject at a time.'

Smoothing out the ball of tissue retrieved from the waste basket, he found the brand of the distillery on it and the words *Cape's Finest Whisky. Bottled in Scotland.* He could see again the shred of tissue found in the bend, with the letters *el* against the ragged right margin. He almost ran to the telephone.

'Lucas, I may have a lead. Find out from the publican if the bottles of whisky sold to Lush that night were wrapped in tissue, and the brand.'

'Right. Hold on. The pub's only across the street.'

Bony's impatience was replaced by the accustomed cold control he exercised over his mind; while waiting he again accused himself of growing old and tired, this time adding the word senile. He could hear a voice, probably from a radio; he heard a rooster crow, and this reminded him of Jill's kookaburras. Waiting, he tried to hear what the voice was saying in the policeman's office. Then the instrument gave a knocking sound, and Lucas began to speak.

'The bottles were sold to Lush with the tissue paper about them. The brand was Skilly's Green Label Irish Whisky. Any use?'

169

'Possibly,' said Bony cautiously. 'Thanks a lot.'

E L were the terminal letters of the word *Label*. The scrap of tissue was so clean and fresh it could have formed part of the wrapper taken off a bottle an hour before he had plucked it from a bush. He remembered that then he had thought it probable that the easterly wind had brought it from the Mira homestead: it could also have been carried by the wind from the camp of The Brothers. It could not have been brought by the wind from the abandoned utility or from Madden's homestead. However, check.

He sought information from Jill.

'From the bottles I've seen lying about, Inspector, Lush drank Irish whisky,' she answered. 'But I've seen Scotch bottles, too, and he must have bought them, because Mother never touched it.'

'Have you noticed the tissue-paper wrappings?'

'Yes. I've seen such paper sometimes.'

'Thanks, Jill. I may be getting warm, as the children say. What are you sewing?'

'I'm making an afternoon-tea apron for Mrs Cosgrove. She asked me if I would, and I said, of course, I'd be glad to do anything.'

'You are a little happier than you were?'

The girl nodded, her eyes bright.

'You are a very kind man,' she said. 'I've heard the others call you Bony. Would you let me?'

'I've been wondering when you would, Jill.'

MacCurdle pulled the men off the job at four o'clock, and he and Ray came in both tired and wet. Bony met them at the door to the private room.

'Could I persuade you?' he asked blandly, and might have been skittled in the rush.

'Two points off three inches,' Ray announced. 'No sign of easing, either.'

'Lucas told me the weather men predict fine for the night.'

'They didn't predict the rain coming, Bony. Anyway, how have you been putting in time?'

'Just pottering about: just pottering. This is good whisky, Mac. D'you ever buy Irish – Skilly's Green Label?'

The Scotchman's sandy eyebrows shot upward.

'I drink Irish?'

'Why not? I'm not a drinker, but I have imbibed Irish whisky and found it very good.'

Still indignant, MacCurdle parried. 'You don't imbibe Irish, Bony. You toss it down fast to by-pass the taste.'

'So we agree that you don't buy Irish?'

'Listen to him, Ray. We work hard in the rain all day, and he starts an argument about Irish whisky.'

'I'm not buying into it, Mac,' Ray said, laughing. Then, to Bony, 'Yes, Mister Holmlock Shears, you may take it for truth that Mac has never bought Irish. Of course, he wouldn't be slow in racing forward if someone offered Irish on a silver salver. You interested in Irish whisky?'

'Yes, I am, Ray. Have you or Mrs Cosgrove purchased Skilly's Green Label? Say, within the last six months?'

'No. I've never seen it here. But there's a good sale for it down at White Bend. Well, I'm for a hot shower and dry clothes.'

MacCurdle's flash of temper had vanished, and he said he would follow suit.

'Before you go, Mac, let me have the weather

records for the past month and this one, will you?'
Bony said. In the outer office he began to study the
sheets which noted wind direction and cloud forma-
tion. He found that the last day on which the wind
came from the west was 10 July, and, from the north-
west, 9 July. The records did not show wind strength.

Over after-dinner coffee Ray brought up the
subject of Irish whisky, and asked why Bony was
interested in it, and because Bony intended to seek
a favour he told them of the scrap of tissue paper
which had come from a bottle similar to one bought
by Lush before leaving town.

'The wind doubtless impaled it on the bush, and
because I could see no other pieces of it, and had cut
no recent human tracks, I permitted myself to assume
that the wind had brought it quite a long way: say
from Mira, or from Madden's homestead, or from the
abandoned utility.

'On the ninth of this month the wind came from
the north-west, and, at the point where I found the
piece of tissue, Madden's homestead would be to the
north-west. The next day the wind came from the
west; that is, from the abandoned utility. Can you
make a guess what the strength of the wind was on
those two days?'

MacCurdle said he thought neither day was very
windy, not as windy as the days when the wind came
from the east and south-east. Ray thought he might
get a clue by referring to the work diary, and
hastened to the office. He returned able to say that
he was right: the diary proved that on the tenth of
the month he and Vickory with two men had tidied
up about the shearing-shed. The rubbish and debris
had been burnt, and he recollected that the smoke

wasn't bothersome, proving that the wind that day was not strong.

'I'm pretty sure it wasn't strong enough either day to carry a bit of tissue to the place you say you saw it, Bony.'

'Do you agree that the east wind was strong enough on other days to carry it there from Mira?' asked Bony.

'Strong enough to carry it, Bony, but the odds laid by the trees and things would be terrific. You say it was clean and new-looking. How d'you think it got there if the wind didn't take it?'

'I dislike offering a wild guess,' Bony replied.

'It's certainly a teasing puzzle,' said Mrs Cosgrove. 'I remember going into that awful place with my husband. Half-dead trees, billabongs which looked like the pits on the moon, banshees peering over fallen logs.'

'I didn't like it, either, Mrs Cosgrove,' said Bony. 'However, I shall have to go again. You have taken the boats from the river. Would you tell me why?'

'They were afloat on the bend hole for so long that we thought it best to get them up and re-pitch them or something of the kind in case we needed them for the flood. Have they been attended to, Mac?'

'They were, Mrs Cosgrove. They're ready to take to the water again.'

'You're not thinking of crossing to Madman's Bend, are you?' Ray asked.

'I have decided to do so, Ray.'

'But the river's in flood. It's full of trees and logs, dangerous enough to sink a ship.'

'I expect I shall manage. Better a boat than swimming,' Bony smilingly announced.

Chapter Twenty-One

A Gamble Pays Off

The kookaburra chortled and cackled; the galahs swooped in flocks of hundreds, chattering and performing aerial feats as though intending to show off their best before the flock broke into the annual mating period; a billion frogs came up to honk, honk, honk. From the flawless sky the sun radiated warmth, bringing a promise of fast growth of grass and herbage on the sandy plains.

Once again Bony stood on the levee and studied the Gutter of Australia. Water was running into the billabong behind the garden. It could be seen running there, the sluggish rivulets giving it animation. The water mass of the river itself slid rather than ran into the wide sweep of the angle, slid round and by Bony, slid on down to pass the shearing-shed and the abandoned camp on the far bank. And this opposite bank, much lower than the Mira side, seemed to be merely four feet above the water.

Like the inner bank at all these bends, the one opposite Mira shelved to the river bed, and there, too, the river had collected white sand to form a spit. This bank would not have been difficult to climb, whereas the steep banks of the reaches, now drenched by rain, would have been as difficult as a greasy pole, and infinitely more dangerous.

The cliff-like bank fringed by the levee was now only twelve feet above the yellowish water. The river continued to carry small masses of debris, larger masses of small branches, and occasionally what seemed to be an entire gum tree. Now and then the metallic surface was broken by logs which had once sunk to the bottom and which the long drying period before the flood had made semi-buoyant. These were rising and sinking, eventually to sink permanently; if they rose under a boat they could fling the occupant into the water. There lay the greatest hazard. To navigate the crossing successfully required only mapping and timing.

Bony weighed the risks against the profits, if any, to his investigation. The risks were evident, the profits nebulous. He had visited the camp abandoned by The Brothers, had poked among the rubbish, but this he had done merely to discover anything that might connect the three men with Lush and his utility. Even if he found a Green Label Whisky bottle he would have no proof of The Brothers' complicity in the murder. They had money to buy tobacco and food· therefore they had money to buy whisky.

However, Bony was being prodded by a sense of urgency and by the prospect of the river itself denying him further opportunity to examine the scene of the crime for signs of the activity of those having possible connection with it. By the coming evening the opposite bank would be submerged, and Madman's Bend merely a tree-studded lake. If he failed to apprehend the killer of William Lush he would most certainly regret not having paid the abandoned camp one more visit.

'You would be foolish to attempt it, Bony,' said Mrs Cosgrove, who was standing beside him. Ray, appearing at his other side, earnestly agreed with her.

'I think it feasible to scull a boat close to the bank up to the place where Lush's body was held,' Bony explained, 'then to row fast across the river, when the current would take the boat downstream and permit a landing on that sand spit over there.'

'Looks feasible, but it's damn dangerous,' Ray said. 'And how do you plan to get back this side again?'

'By the return route. Up along that far bank, then cross to be swept down to land where I started.'

'Just why do you want to do it?' asked Mrs Cosgrove. 'What d'you hope to find over there?'

'Something missed at my last visit.'

'But no sure purpose?'

Bony sighed, shrugged, and fell to making a cigarette.

'I have a long record of crime-investigation successes,' he said, so softly that he might have been talking to himself. 'The record is founded on patience, tenacity, observation. I've had a great ally, time. Should I fail in this particular investigation, no one is going to concede that it was the river which defeated me. That will be bad enough, but what will be far worse is that I myself will know that, had I not feared this day, I would have crossed and might have found a clue to add another success to the total. So I must cross, or never want to see myself again in a shaving-mirror.'

'Then the sooner you make the attempt the better,'

young Cosgrove said. 'Help me with the boat. We can manage.'

'I shall not stay to watch,' said Mrs Cosgrove, and left them.

Ray led Bony to a near-by shed, where the two boats lay bottoms-up on trestles. He advised Bony to take the smaller craft, saying it was the easier to row, and this they turned over to rest on a wheeled carriage.

'Better take an extra oar, Bony. You might lose one. Never know how it will turn out.'

The boat was launched below the pumping-engine slipway, and Ray turned it about to grasp it by the stern and allow Bony to step in.

'You know how to row, I suppose?' the young man taunted him. 'Take a mug's advice and face the bow and push at the oars. You can see where to go.'

Now that he was about to begin the crossing, Bony's depression lifted.

'I'll be all right,' he called over a shoulder, and shipped the oars. 'Push me off, and thank you.'

He felt the stern sink lower with the forward movement, then felt the craft shudder, and heard a splash. Thinking that Ray had fallen in, he was about to whirl the boat about when Cosgrove said:

'Full speed ahead, Bony, or we'll be taken into the billabong.'

'You idiot! What are you in the boat for?'

' 'Cos you can't row close to the bank with your starboard oar out. I can feather-scull over the stern, and keep it hard against the bank.'

When they had passed the inlet to the billabong Bony was ordered to unship his oars; turning, he berated his companion, who was standing and calmly moving the craft within a foot of the steep and greasy bank.

'Shut up, Bony. I'm the captain of this ship. Save your breath for oar-pushing. You'll want it.'

'Lunatic!' shouted Bony, really angry. 'Mrs Cosgrove will be furious with me for allowing you to take risks without possible reason. We'll put back. Turn the boat around.'

'You attend to your duties, sir. So far we're doing nicely.'

Bony surrendered. It was too late to turn back. He was conscious of the bank slowly passing on the one side and an enormous tree passing on the other, its branches seemingly reaching for the cockleshell. Inactivity was beginning to attack him when Ray asked did he think this was far enough up-river to make the crossing.

'What do you think?' he countered, sensibly admitting that the young man had had far more experience than he.

'This will do. Let's see what's coming first. Right! All clear, bar the rising submarines. Now push like hell.'

Bony pushed like hell, and Ray feathered hard to keep the bow slightly up-river. The current took them, and the trees on the far bank seemed miles away and determinedly marching up-river. Ray began to whistle the 'Jolly Swagman' to a march beat. Then Bony's starboard oar scraped on something harder than water, and up beside them rose a 'submarine'. Fortunately they found themselves on the right side of it, and when Bony again dipped the oar the log had sunk.

Cheerfully, Cosgrove shouted, 'See what I mean,

Bony. Good enough to sink a battleship. Lash into it, old pal. Only another ten or twelve miles to go.' A mass of tree bark entwined about a buoyant branch bore down upon them, and Ray had to turn the bow of the boat directly upstream to permit it to pass between them and the bank. The bank was now some fifty yards ahead of them.

When they entered the narrow strip of backwater against the bank Bony was thankful for many small mercies and convinced he would never have made the crossing without Ray Cosgrove's powerful assistance. With his feathering oar astern, the young man took the boat downstream to the upper 'shore' of the sand spit and held the bow against it.

Bony tossed the anchor to dry land, jumped from the boat, and hauled it high to permit Ray to join him.

'Nice going, Bony. We've earned a fag.'

'And we have an audience, Ray.'

On the levee stood the cook and Jacko and Mrs Cosgrove. They were too far off for their expressions to be seen, but the young man offered a guess when he said with mock childishness, 'My muvver is gonna go crook when I gets 'ome.'

'Serve you right. She is entitled to,' Bony said, severely. 'I'm not ungrateful, but I cannot commend your action. Most certainly I would not have agreed to it. Now let us take a little walk.'

They went up to the summit of the bank, and there they could see water amid the trees inside the bend. Almost at once they saw a carpet snake some eight feet long; they were to see many others of various species, from diamond to black snakes, aroused by the creeping water.

Arming themselves with sticks, they proceeded under the line of red-gums, the debris of which made walking easy; beyond was deep mud. They could hear the noise of the machines away from the shearing-shed, and, as no one sat or stood by the fireplace, Bony presumed that Dead March Harry and his mate were working.

At the site of the bedraggled, vacated camp Bony asked Ray to sit on a log and be silent while he wandered about and concentrated on reading a story from the rain-soaked ground. As previously noted, the rough-cut poles proved that each of The Brothers had stretched a sheet to form an inverted V to give shelter in case of rain, and beneath these Vs each had formed a thick mattress of leaves. It was a universal practice with men intending to camp more than one night.

Now Bony kicked these leaf mattresses asunder, hoping that one of The Brothers might have pushed something of value among them and forgotten it. There was nothing. He saw two other such mattresses and kicked those to pieces, too; then he realized that above these were no poles. Five men had been camping here, two in addition to The Brothers. He would have to ascertain which of the ten they were.

The Brothers had not been unmindful of the ants; they had tossed bottles and tins into a shallow hole some dozen yards from the camp, and here Bony found tomato and Worcester sauce bottles outnumbering a few spirit bottles and several beer bottles.

Bony called to Ray and asked if the bottles of Irish whisky were stamped with the distiller's name. He was told that they were, and he found no bottle stamped by Skilly. This dump had been visited by a dog since the rain. The easterlies had carried sheets of newspaper and the well-remembered outside cover sheet of the *Bulletin* against bush and trees, and much of it still remained despite the downpour. Of tissue wrapping paper there was not a shred.

'Find anything?' Ray asked when Bony sat with him, smoking.

'Nothing of significance. However, there were five men, not three, camped here. The Brothers had two guests.'

'Pity! Had our little row for nothing. Still, it was a break from work.'

'You mightn't think so on the way back.'

'Oh, we'll get back all right,' said Ray with the assurance of youth. 'Crikey, look at that!'

It was a small dog of very mixed ancestry. It stood looking at them from the rubbish dump, and its tail was wagging slowly as though its owner were doubtful of the two men. At Ray's sharp whistle the tail flagged relief, and the animal advanced, venting low moans of pleasure. Her flanks were tucked in by hunger.

'The Brothers must have left her behind,' Ray said, and clicked his fingers to encourage the dog further. She came right to him, and turned herself into the shape of an S.

'She's suckling pups – probably has them hidden and wouldn't leave without them.'

Ray began to speak to the dog as though she could understand English, asking about her pups, where they were. Bony started off on another inspection of the camp and, having the dog in mind, sought and found no meat bones. He was aware that the dog was trotting into the bend and that Ray Cosgrove was following her. He teased the mattresses again, and his

181

persistence was rewarded even as Ray shouted for him to join him.

Picking up the unexploded ·32 cartridge, he pocketed it and went through the leaves with his hands to scatter them thoroughly. Finding nothing further, he joined Cosgrove at the end of a wind-severed tree branch. The absence of meat bones at the camp was explained by the numerous well-gnawed bones about the branch.

'She's got her pups in there,' Ray said, pointing to the splintered end of the branch. 'You can hear them. I've reached in, but I can't touch one.'

'A problem to get them out. We can't leave them or the mother here.' Bony was obliged to force his mind from the cartridge and the two additional men to this pups problem. 'Now if we only had a length of fencing wire.'

'Fencing wire! If that's all we need there's an old fence down-river a bit. How much do we want?'

'About a couple of yards to make sure. Bring it, and I'll try to coax the mother out again.'

Ray Cosgrove departed for the wire, and Bony squatted and whistled cheerfully, fondling the cartridge in his pocket.

Chapter Twenty-Two

The Unappreciated Rescue

Bony was holding the dog when Ray returned with the wire.

'I don't want to use the wire save as a last resort, Ray. Think we could up-end the branch so that the pups would fall out?'

'No skin off our noses to try.'

'We cannot free this lady, and we've nothing to tie on to her. Bar that wire. You hold the dog.'

Had the animal worn a collar the task would have been simple. The wire was old but still stiff. Eventually Bony managed to form a knot which could not slip, and she was attached to another branch.

Their efforts to raise the branch failed. It was necessary to smoke a cigarette before putting the ultimate plan into execution.

'Now we'll have to be cruel to be kind, as your great-great-grandmother probably said more than once,' Bony decided. 'This entire bend area will be under water by tomorrow. You'll have to hold the bitch fast, because the pups are going to yell.'

'I see now how you'll operate, Bony. Yes, she'll struggle for sure.'

The wire was removed from the dog, and Bony

straightened it and selected a jagged end. Lying full length on the ground, he inserted the wire into the hollow branch and gently felt with it. He could hear the animal inside and when one yelped with surprise he held the end of the wire against it and slowly twisted. The jagged end became enmeshed in hair, and when the pup was strongly protesting Bony was able to draw it from the branch. Its eyes were not yet open.

Meanwhile the mother was frantic. She quietened a little when given the pup. Bony's second attempt was not as quickly successful; there was strong protest before he succeeded. Numbers three and four were brought out yelling their heads off. Number five seemed to be playing hide-and-seek with the end of the wire, and it took half an hour of prospecting to capture it.

'I can hear no more,' Bony said. 'Any hurt?'

'One's got a bit of hide off, and two are scratched somewhat. That's a neat trick.'

'A lubra first adopted it to get a rabbit from a blind hole. Trust the blacks to invent ways to avoid hard work. Over in West Australia they don't go to all the trouble of running a meat trail and laying poison baits for foxes; then they'd have to get up at first light to defeat the crows before they tear at the skin. Father Abo sits off the burrow with a shot-gun, and Mother Abo sneaks on to the burrow and coughs down a hole. She creeps away, and the fox comes up to see what made that strange noise.'

'They're trumps, Bony, old shipmate. Where do we go from here?'

By now the dog was pacified, and between them they carried the pups to the boat. Ray said that

MacCurdle would go crook on him for bringing back five useless mongrel pups to grow into sheep-killers.

'They just couldn't be kelpies or border collies,' he said. 'They just had to be mongrels. Probably have to shoot 'em. Well, Mac can do that. I couldn't after the trouble of getting them out.'

They were sitting on the bank, damp as it was, and the dog was feeding her pups. Bony was again absorbed by the river.

'The water's changing colour,' he said, 'or am I imagining it?'

'You're right. It is. It's getting reddish. I know – it'll be the water from Red Creek. Runs the colour of blood. The audience is on again.'

On the other bank was the men's cook in his white apron, and with him were Jacko and Vickory and several others. Bony sought the sun's position.

'After twelve, Ray. Lunch time. Shall we push off?'

'Might as well.'

With the dogs in the bow, and Bony sitting facing them and ready to ship his oars, Ray propelled the boat up-river, hugging the bank. He was aware of a grave difficulty to be overcome. Two hundred yards above the sand spit there was a protuberance of the bank about which the main river current was strong. At this point there was no reverse 'shore' current. Coming down-river it was easy to navigate this miniature headland. Now approaching it Ray pointed out that the current might take charge of the bow, swing it outward and take them downstream.

'I could use an oar to help,' Bony shouted, and thrust the outside oar into the rowlock.

Without the oar work the current might have won. They went higher up-river to make the crossing, and for a moment or two studied the surface, and then waited for several ugly masses of flotsam to pass by, and observed two wallowing 'submarines'.

The crossing was made, and again Bony was thankful that young Cosgrove was with him. Eventually they were welcomed by the audience.

Mrs Cosgrove glared at Bony and berated her son. Vickory asked why they were such lunatics, and snorted when Bony told them that he had heard a dog barking on the opposite side, had seen the dog was fearful of the rising flood, and had merely gone over to rescue it.

'It's our dog,' claimed a bearded man Bony knew to be one of The Brothers. 'Disappeared three-four days before we left camp.'

'Well, get rid of the pups, Silas. Pity you brought 'em back, Inspector.'

'We couldn't leave them after she led us to them in a hollow tree branch,' said Bony quietly. The Cosgroves had gone off to the house; The Brothers took their dog and the pups, and Bony never subsequently inquired after them.

Before lunch Mrs Cosgrove asked to be forgiven for blaming him about her son, who had admitted he had tricked Bony into taking him on the voyage.

'Actually, I am very glad he did, Mrs Cosgrove, because I don't think I would have made it alone. I was angry when I found him in the boat, but . . . By the way, did you happen to mention why I wished to cross?'

'No.' She smiled in that tight manner which gave him cause to wonder whether she was still furious with him. 'Your story to the men was rather thin, don't you think?'

'I thought it was rather good,' Bony said, laughingly. 'Better a thin one than none. And you should be proud of Ray. He's quite dauntless.'

'I am proud of him. As you say, he's utterly fearless. But neither of you should have taken such risks. You gave me a bad time, but I hope you found it worth while.'

'Yes, I did.' Bony beamed at her. 'We rescued the dogs.'

'Bony, sometimes you resemble my husband. He used to speak provokingly like that. I am glad, however, that your venture was profitable. My, we must go in to lunch.'

Before MacCurdle went out again Bony asked for a spare map of the local area, and was supplied with a large-scale map of the Darling Basin. All the station homesteads were marked, as well as the crossings, whether by bridge or ferry. Against the homestead of Markham Downs he printed: *Jacko during vital period until next day*. Against Murrimundi he printed: *D. M. Harry and Mick-Warder*. Then he rang up Constable Lucas.

'When next you see the mailman ask him if he delivered goods to the men called The Brothers. Could be anything. Say within the last four months. Then inquire at the general store as to whom they sold ·32 calibre cartridges, throughout the same period. Anything for me?'

'Not much so far. On the night in question Wally Watts called for a handout at the Dunlop kitchen, and the Paroo Bikeman was seen camped at the shearing-shed at the Crossing on the night before the vital period covering the Lush murder. I haven't been able to trace Bosun Dean and Champion so far, but I'll keep trying.'

'Thanks, Lucas. It's a nice contribution.'

'How's the flood up there? The rain will raise it more. How much did you get?'

'A few points over four inches,' Bony replied.

'Same here. Break up of the dry spell, all right.'

On this note they severed connection. On his map Bony printed *Wally Watts* against Dunlop homestead, and the *Paroo Bikeman* against the Crossing. The placing of the last-named man was interesting. The Crossing was sixty miles up-river from Mira; the distance would be nothing to the Paroo Bikeman, who might well have been camped near the scene of the crime when it was committed. The Dunlop homestead was approximately twenty-five miles up-river, and it seemed unlikely that Wally Watts would have covered that mileage in one day, big and powerful though he was. To tramp twenty-five miles in a day a man would need to have a distinct objective, and none of these no-hopers was at all likely to be so energetic.

Leaving the office, Bony sauntered to the pumping-plant and there noticed that the water was running more swiftly into the billabong, and that it was clearly tinged with red. The river seemed crowded with debris, probably floated into the main stream down the rain-flooded major creeks.

The men's cook was preparing the afternoon smoko which someone would take in a truck to the workers at the levee.

'Come on in and have a drinker tea, Inspector,' said the cook. 'Whatcher think of the old Gutter? By the morning she'll be as red as blood. Come down like that three years ago, but she wasn't in flood. Clear as rine water one minute: red the next.'

'Comes from Red Creek, they say. More rubbish on it, too.'

The cook paused in packing brownie cake into a carton.

'Crikey! You and young Ray took a chance. I wouldn't be rowing a boat out there for a million quid. Made me sea-sick lookin' at you. No wonder the Missus blew up at Ray.'

He was a solid man, and Bony knew he was called Fred. As he passed from the kitchen to flog his iron triangle, Bony noticed the flat feet in carpet slippers, and the hairless heavy head. Returning, he poured himself a pannikin of tea and refilled Bony's.

'Jacko about?' asked Bony.

'I lets 'im off from three to five. Decent sort of bloke. 'Course, most of these no-hopers are all right. I've done a bit of tramping in me time. I suppose we all has. Got to see what's round the next bend.'

'That's true,' Bony said. 'I find myself that way sometimes. Now I want the answers to a question or two.'

'Try me and I does what I please, eh?'

'Were there any swagmen camped down by the shed that night Lush abandoned his ute?'

'That I couldn't answer. I can say that old Peter Petersen poked his head in through the door in the middle of the afternoon, and I went crook 'cos I was havin' a shut-eye for five minutes. I told him it wasn't the time, and he said he'd been out of tucker since the day before. If he camped here that night, or which way he was travelling, I don't know.'

A motor was heard approaching, and Fred tossed

tea into two new buckets, added boiling water, and stood them by the door. The vehicle was stopped and a man came in for the afternoon smoko; the truck roared away with it. The cook sat again, and loaded a pipe.

'Did The Brothers do much shooting over at their camp?' asked Bony casually.

'Don't think so. Never heard any firing. Blokes on tramp don't usually have rifles with 'em. Too much to hike with without taking on a rifle. Have a few fishing-lines, though. Lines come in handy. Only time I had a gun was when I pushed a bike. Pack a hell of a load on a bike, you know. Knoo a bloke who always pushed one with the pedals off.'

'Well, no one will be fishing for a long time, by the look of the river.'

'That's so, Inspector. But when the flood goes down and the bends run dry the water left in the billabong will soon clear and the fish'll be asking to be hooked. I got a twenty-seven-pounder cod in a billabong once. Then Petersen come along, and we lives on fish for a week. Got starved for mutton, and I took a cooking job on Netley.'

Bony maintained interest in fishing for several minutes before steering the cook round to Petersen.

'How old? Oh, something like sixty. Ain't as old as he looks. Pretty good blacksmith. Could get work any time, any place, but he's kept to the track for the last ten years. Decent old coot. Able to use himself once. I did hear he has a revolver. I've never seen it, but blokes have said he owns one. Always travels alone, and that ain't healthy, so a gun could come handy like. You gets tough characters along this river during the shearing.'

'Locals?'

'Locals! Crikey, the locals is all right! It's the city blokes follering the sheds. Course, there's some tough nuts you might call locals, but not mean. The shearin' being just over, it could have been a city tramp what skittled Lush.'

Chapter Twenty-Three

Strong Suspects

Bony added the name Peter Petersen to his map, and he was still in the office when the men knocked off work and the manager came in.

'I'd like to be a detective, my word I would!' he said dryly. 'Going for boat-rowing in the morning and lolling about all afternoon. I doubt you deserve a snifter. Why didn't you help yourself?'

'I haven't felt like it, Mac. How did your day go?'

'Hard. The mullock's heavy with moisture, and the work's slow.'

'Have you been bossed?'

'Not today. I had to be firm yesterday.' The Scotsman smiled. 'I'd have made a good husband, but I've never been one. Yesterday I thought the men would walk off the job. This morning she increased the bonus. She rattled it into Ray, though, for cruising with you.'

'It was well for me that he stowed away and worked his passage. I could have got into serious difficulty.'

MacCurdle sipped his whisky before venturing to ask, 'Was the trip worth the risks?'

'Yes, it was, Mac. I made a step or two. By the way, have you heard The Brothers shooting about their camp or in the bend?'

'Not that I can recall. Why?'

'Do you sell cartridges here?'

'No. Never stock them.'

'Would other homesteads do so?'

'I wouldn't think so. You see, a homestead store wouldn't stock clothes and personal items; that is, along this river. Well out west on the border they might want to trade with the Aborigines, and cartridges would be in stock. Not to sell to the Abos: to white stockmen and others.'

Bony refrained from saying that he knew the conditions out west, and began on another subject.

'Have you ever found at the mail-box letters deposited by someone else, or letters left there by the mailman for someone not working at Mira?'

'Yes, but seldom. The last time it was a letter for Silas Wishart. Couple of days later there was a letter waiting for the mailman.'

'What of parcels, Mac?'

'No parcels.'

'You are being patient. Just one more thing. The Brothers have been in camp on the other side for several weeks. I think that odd. Men on tramp invariably keep on the move. Can you explain it?'

'There's no particular reason, I think,' MacCurdle replied. 'They're peculiar men in that one won't work without the other two. They worked through the shearing for Mira, then spent a couple or three days down at the White Bend pub, and came up here to camp where they did. That side belongs to Murrimundi, but, as you must have seen, the entire area is useless, and as the men have never been bothersome we can't object to them camping.'

The telephone rang. MacCurdle said the call was for Bony, and departed. Lucas reported that the store-keeper had been most co-operative, and he read from a list of names persons supplied with ·32 calibre cartridges. On the list were William Lush and Raymond Cosgrove. Lucas said he knew all the customers, and officially had nothing against any one of them.

Regarding parcels, the policeman reported that the mail driver had on two occasions delivered a parcel consigned to The Brothers, and that in each instance one of them waited on the track about a mile south of the Mira box. One parcel was sent by the publican, who remembered filling an order for half a dozen bottles of whisky, and the other contained a pair of boots and three shirts. Finally, Lucas had three names for Bony's map. Bosun Dean was camped at the Murrimundi shearing-shed, and Champion and a man called Miner Smith were seen fishing at a bend hole two miles north of Murrimundi on the opposite side.

Having added these names to the map, Bony could find no pointer to the killer of William Lush. All of them with the exception of Wally Watts – for he had only Jacko's word that he had stayed over at Markham Downs – could reasonably be suspected. Yet another suspect was Raymond Cosgrove, and Bony decided to test him.

After dinner he asked the young man to accompany him to MacCurdle's private room; there he shut the door and abruptly began the inquisition.

'Do you happen to own a ·32 calibre rifle?'

'Yes, I do. Want to borrow it?'

'If you have no objection,' Bony said. 'I'd like to fire half a dozen bullets from it and submit those bullets to our ballistics people.'

'All right, shipmate.' Ray's smile was open; then it vanished as his eyes widened. 'You are thinking I shot Lush?'

'I believe it's possible you shot Lush. There are several men who could have shot him, but to date I can apply no motive to any one of them. You could have had a motive. You had opportunity. And since you own a rifle of the same calibre as that which killed Lush, you had the means.

'First: motive. You are in love with Jill, and she with you. You are thought to have been the first to find the abandoned ute. You could have found Lush tinkering with it, and what you knew of his violent assaults on his wife and threats to Jill could have prompted you to shoot him and toss the body over the cliff. In that you had opportunity. You certainly had the means.'

'But that's all bloody rot!' asserted Ray, eyes blazing.

'Of course it is,' said Bony calmly. 'It's why I want to borrow your rifle, and if others of the same calibre are here, then those as well. Are there any others?'

'No other thirty-two here. Vickory has one.'

'Very well. Tomorrow I'll take specimen bullets from yours. Meanwhile, have you at any time given or sold some of your cartridges to anyone?'

Ray shook his head.

'Would you know if one or more had been taken from your stock?'

'Yes. Yes, I would. I blew out of 'em, and got a

195

fresh supply from White Bend only two weeks ago.
I haven't opened a box.'

'Bring them here, and the rifle, too, please.'

Thoughtfully rolling a cigarette, Bony felt sure he
had come to yet another dead end, for he could detect
no defence blockage, no hidden current of opposition,
in this boyish young man. Ray brought the rifle,
which was beautifully kept, and three boxes of
cartridges corresponding with Lucas's report of the
purchase.

'No one borrowed this weapon?' he asked, and
knew the answer before it was given. 'Tell me, have
you heard any shooting by The Brothers? Anyone
else?'

Ray said he hadn't heard shooting for months, and
then it had been Lush hunting in Madman's Bend.

'You think it possible I could have shot him?'

'Possible, but improbable. Are you aware that
there were two men camped with The Brothers?'

'No. But now you mention it I remember that you
spoke of five men this morning.'

'I started on this case too early,' Bony said, eyes
directed to his shoes. 'When I first visited that camp
on the day the flood came down I was almost convinced that Lush was alive because I was almost
convinced that Jill's bullet through the door hadn't
killed him. I am certainly baffled, and admit it. You
have often been in mind as the killer, and I trust you
will understand why.'

'I understand it, Bony. As you said, I had motive,
I had opportunity, and I had the means. Come to
sum it up, to suspect me is your job. There's no bad
feeling about it.'

'I am glad you said that, Ray. I may again call for

this rifle, but I shall hope not. D'you know of anyone
on Mira who owns a revolver or pistol?'

'I don't think anyone does. We'd have no use for
one.'

'Can you tell me anything of a man named Peter
Petersen?' Bony persisted, and was given the smell
of oil, if not a strike.

'Old Petersen! Yes, I know him. I was talking to
him only a few days ago.'

'The day before Lush disappeared?' asked Bony
sharply.

'Yes. It was in the afternoon,' replied Ray. 'He was
boiling his billy at the shearing-shed. Used to work
here sometimes, and I asked him how he was coming
along.'

'And he said——?'

'Said he was keeping all right. He said, too, he was
headed for a job. I must have looked a bit doubtful,
because then he told me he'd heard that his married
daughter in Adelaide was sick and up against it. The
daughter once worked with her husband for us, but
he died, and Petersen was worried.'

'Did he say where this job was?'

'Yes. For the Vospers. They have a place eight to
nine miles out west from Madden's. In fact, they've
taken over Jill's sheep.'

'These Vospers would be on the telephone, of
course?'

Ray nodded, and Bony rose to ask the White Bend
exchange to put him through. Ray could hear him
speaking.

'Mr Vosper? I am Inspector Bonaparte ringing
from Mira. Have you taken on a man named Petersen? You have. When?'

'On the twentieth of this month, Inspector.'

'He would have arrived at your place the day before, I take it?'

'He did that. What can we do for you?'

'I rather want to talk with him, but the river fetters me. I could have Constable Lucas deputize for me, but I don't wish to bother him. I wonder, now, would you see Petersen, and ask him confidentially if he still carries a pistol or revolver, and ascertain the calibre.'

'Of course, Inspector. It'll be serious for him if he does, won't it?'

'That's why I don't want to bother Lucas. Lucas will probably be ringing you to ask what swagmen camped or called round about the time Lush vanished, and you need not mention my interest in Petersen. Could you obtain the information for me tonight?'

'Certainly. I'll ring you back.'

Bony returned to the inner room, saying to the expectant young Cosgrove, 'Can I rely on you to forget what you've heard?'

'I'll not repeat any of it, Bony. None of my business.'

'Good! Now tell me this. What kind of man is this Petersen? Bad-tempered, argumentative?'

'I don't think either. He's a blacksmith. As I said, he's worked for us lots of times. Quiet man. No, he never argued about anything. Of course, he's getting on. Must be over sixty. What would he want with a pistol? He's harmless enough.'

'Yet he would encounter on the track men who are not harmless.' Bony rolled a cigarette, studied the young man, glanced at the clock. 'What time of day was it you saw Petersen?'

'About three-ish.'

'Did he say where he intended to camp that night?'

'No. He hadn't unrolled his swag, so I can't give a pointer.'

'It's more than likely that he did camp that night at the shearing-shed. The next day, the day that the utility was found at the boxes, he arrived at the Vospers'. Sometimes I err. I proffer an assumption when I ought to be explicit. If Petersen stayed the night here, then he would have seen the utility the following morning, the utility being on the route from Mira to Vospers'. Now why didn't I cut his tracks in the vicinity of that utility?'

'Easy answer, Bony. He was wearing rubber-soled tennis shoes. Always does. Those on him were worn. Ground was hard and the wind at the boxes would have blown out the tracks on the soft ground.'

'I am not excused.'

He relapsed into meditation, and Ray took up a stock journal. Thirty minutes passed, then the phone called. Vosper said, 'I tackled Petersen, Inspector. He admits carrying a .32 calibre pistol, and says he's had no cartridges for it for more than a year.'

Chapter Twenty-Four

The Ponderous Enemy

Disturbing reports of the river were received the next morning, and Mrs Cosgrove with MacCurdle worked to assess the extent of the danger to Mira. The main crest of the flood could be expected ten days hence, but added to the course of the steady rise would be the run-off from the recent rain. Hope lay in the possibility that the run-off might pass Mira before its influence could disastrously affect the main crest. If the two coincided the levee might well fail to hold it.

'Those three men out back with the sheep had better be brought in,' suggested the manager. 'The sheep being off the river country will be all right, but we could get the Wilga people to send one of their men to check if we're flood-bound longer than a fortnight.'

'Very well, send for them,' assented the owner.

'Good! Then Ray had better go straightaway.'

'See to it, Mac. I'll get the latest weather map.'

Mrs Cosgrove contacted Superintendent Macey.

'Ah! Good morning, Betsy! How's your flood?'

'Going to be worse before it's better. What says the latest weather chart?'

'I thought you'd want that, so I rang Dubbo as they

get the paper very early. The chart's a dry one. The central point of a high is placed at Kalgoorlie, and there's nothing in front to worry you. Could arrive at this longitude in forty-eight hours.'

'Is there a following low?'

'No, but the rear isobars indicate a low west of Port Hedland. Too far away for worry. More than fifteen hundred miles away.'

'Thanks, Jim. Keep an eye on that distant low. It could bring a strong westerly, and Mac's afraid it might raise waves from this long reach to smash against the levee.'

'It could, too. I'll get tomorrow's weather map from Dubbo, first thing. How is our friend progressing? Keeping you all cheerful, I hope.'

'I cannot say anything of his progress,' reported Mrs Cosgrove. 'He took a river trip yesterday in the smaller of our boats. Went tramping about on the other side. That idiot of a Ray went with him. Why they weren't upset and drowned I'll never know. Mac asked him whether the trip had been profitable, and he said it had. Nothing more than that, Jim. Oh yes, they brought a mongrel dog and her five puppies back with them. As though we haven't enough dogs to feed.'

Macey chuckled, saying that if Bony was happy doodling about the place everyone should be happy, too.

'Tell him, Betsy, that his Commissioner is getting cranky, and that he could be sacked once again and for keeps.'

'And you tell his Commissioner that he's marooned and could be that way for a month or two.'

While this chit-chat was going on Bony was standing

on the levee gazing upon the Gutter. The water was light red in colour. The level was only five to six feet below the edge of the near bank. The opposite bank had disappeared, and the bordering gums stood in water. Madman's Bend was carrying water from the upper bend right across it: actually there were now no bends, and because of this release from confinement the river itself was running comparatively sluggish. Its rise, too, was now slower.

The men at work this morning were beyond the shed, and the noise of the machines reverberated between the red-gums. Bony heard also the light truck being driven by Ray for the reinforcements. It was another brilliant day, the wind cold from the south, the scents of the revivified earth sweet and alluring. Who would want to be a city cop?

Bony was becoming uneasy about this case, for his old ally, time, was being defeated by the Gutter of Australia raising the water to wash out for ever the clues and leads that the ground would have contained.

Even normal procedure was now upset by the flood. He should question The Brothers about the two recent visitors to their camp, although he gravely doubted that they would reveal who the two were. They are very close, these men of the outback tracks, and to question them without at least the probability of being told the truth would be unwise.

He decided to reverse his approach to Peter Petersen, and he strode to the office and phoned Lucas. Having said where Petersen was to be found, he asked the policeman if he could go there.

'Yes, the track's above flood level,' replied Lucas. 'Doesn't touch the river anywhere. I could go out this morning.'

'I need to know when Petersen left the Mira shed, and the exact route he took almost step by step. I want to know who he met, if anyone, and if he passed the utility, and the time. He owns a thirty-two revolver, and he told Vosper he had had no cartridges for it for over a year. Take the revolver, fire bullets from it and send them to Ballistics by the best route open to you. Meanwhile don't charge him with possession. Tell him so. Use him gently. It could pay.'

'All right, I'll go to it,' replied Lucas. 'I was coming to checking the Vospers' selection. There's two others for your list, or rather a correction. I reported yesterday that Champion and Miner Smith were seen fishing two miles above Murrimundi homestead. I've learned subsequently that they were camped in the hut at the Murrimundi wool-scour plant on the night in question.'

'Wait, please,' Bony snapped, and referred to his map. On the line again, he asked, 'Where is the man Smith now?'

'Here in town, or was an hour ago.'

'Good! Question him before going to Vospers'. Who else was camped at that scour? Who did he see that day? Be crafty, Lucas. Much could depend on his information.'

'I get it, Bony. I'll ring you back.'

Bony stepped to the veranda and sat on an old chair, from which vantage he could see the levee beyond the pumping-plant, see it extending past the men's quarters. The bulldozer was pushing earth against the levee, and men with shovels were tossing it to the top, where other men were spreading and tramping it hard.

Mrs Cosgrove came up the steps, and he offered the chair to her.

'I saw you sitting here, Bony, and I wish to tell you I was talking with Superintendent Macey. Just gossiping, you know. He asked if you had made any progress. Have you?'

'The progress made is about the distance between the point where a jumping ant takes off and the point of its landing.' He smiled a trifle grimly. 'I assume that Macey told you that my superiors are becoming impatient.'

'He implied it, and he seemed resigned about it.'

'I am being tempted by this river to be impatient, too, Mrs Cosgrove. It has driven me from the scene of the crime. It has frustrated me in several ways. However, the man wanted could be working on that levee this morning.'

'Oh! If he is, you will be arresting him?'

'Not till the flood recedes and leaves Mira safe. You'll want his labour, I'm sure.'

'Of course we shall. Mac sent Ray off to bring in the outside men. We'll need every man possible.'

'Then you may count on me, although my hands are very soft. Ah! I'm expecting a call.'

It was Lucas reporting.

'Smith says he and Champion were camped at the scour the day before Lush vanished, the day he did vanish and the following day. He gave me no reason to doubt that during their stay they saw no one. In case you don't know, the place is inside a bend and almost a mile off the road. Any good?'

'Offers a lead, Lucas. Thanks. Now for Petersen, please.'

Mrs Cosgrove smiled when he joined her to sit on

the floor of the veranda and employ his fingers with
tobacco and paper.

'So you've been offered a lead?' she said.

'Eavesdropper,' he said with a smile.

'Shameless, Bony. You know, I think women would
be better detectives than men. They are more un-
scrupulous.'

'Heaven forbid!' he exclaimed. 'I would be un-
employed.'

'Well, come along in for morning tea, and we can
argue the pros and cons. Yes! When I came out from
England I disapproved strongly of this incessant tea-
drinking, but I became another slave to it. Some
Americans visited us and were horrified by the cups
of tea we drank throughout the day. My husband
teasingly told them we were out of coffee, and they
told us we were savages. We didn't even provide
drinking water on the table. That was my husband's
fault. Water! A man wasn't a sheep or a horse,' he
said.

'They, and you when you first came, must have
found our Australian ways often disconcerting,' Bony
commented. 'Still, we have our good points. We never
run, but always arrive.'

Jill Madden was in the breakfast-room, and she
poured the tea. This morning she was almost
vivacious.

'I saw you coming, and brought the smoko as Emma
is busy,' she said. 'I've been down to the river. It
looks . . . it looks grand, I think. I wonder if it'll
enter home.'

'It's never done so before,' Mrs Cosgrove said, and
to Bony it appeared of no importance to Jill if it did.
He opened the subject of Petersen.

'Poor old chap, he often worked here,' said Mrs Cosgrove. 'Hearing his blacksmith's hammer on the anvil reminded me of home when I stayed with relatives in a small Sussex village. I haven't seen him for months.'

'He's working for the Vospers,' Bony said. Mrs Cosgrove raised her brows. 'I've been using your telephone when you were not sitting on the veranda.'

'Mercy! The mind never sleeps!'

'I've learned that he has a daughter who is very ill, and needs money. Has he a daughter?'

'Of course. She and her husband were once employed here.'

'Can you remember when you last saw him, Jill?'

'He hasn't come to our place for months,' she replied.

'Can you tell me what kind of a man he is? Manner, not appearance?'

'Oh, Petersen's harmless. Always polite. Always grateful for what Mother gave him.'

'Is he a suspect, Bony?' asked Mrs Cosgrove. Bony smiled mysteriously. 'You policemen! I suppose it's the way you are trained.'

'We were taught very early to impress people with knowing far more than we do. All great men conceal ignorance beneath an easy smile. And now, if you will permit, I'd like to look at the river and meditate.'

'And I have letters to write,' his hostess declared. 'Ray will be taking the mail down to Murrimundi this afternoon.'

'Then I will write to my wife. She worries if I don't report regularly.'

Bony wrote:

The Ponderous Enemy

Sweetheart!

As always you are seldom excluded from my thoughts, and should I be unable to write for a few weeks be assured it will be due to the Darling, which is flowing strongly, and will soon become a giant. The Darling River is not always a darling. As at present it is a ponderous Goliath, and this giant is the thing with which I am in conflict. Hitherto the opposing force has been human in weaknesses which, with the aid of time, I have been able to overcome.

Now time has deserted me, and the river has submerged the infinite pieces of the story I began to read and could not progress beyond the second chapter. It promised to be a most interesting story, too. It began with a bullet through a door, the door broken by an axe, and the axe lying on the ground outside. The character thought to be the axe-wielder was known to be a violent man, much disliked by everybody, and the circumstances seemed to indicate temporary retirement into the bush with a supply of liquor. Then the wife he had attacked died, and it became a case of homicide. Efforts by others to find him matched my own frustration when tracking him. Then he turned up dead in the rising river with a bullet hole in his head, and this bullet was subsequently proved not to have been fired through the door.

By now you will be exasperated, not because you are minus our inherited attribute of patience, but with me for teasing your curiosity, which we also inherited.

Dear Marie, be not concerned about me. This homestead is commodious and occupies the centre of a luscious garden. The owner is a Mrs Cosgrove, an English woman of education and some charm, and of discernment concerning me. Her son, Ray, is very like our little Ed, who would be a year or two older. He is in love with the daughter of the dead woman, and I wish we had a daughter like her.

However, we must both continue to be grateful for our children. When Little Ed chooses to marry, I could retire and we could build a house on this beautiful river, and go on walkabouts, and recall all the struggles and all the little triumphs we have shared since that time I pinched your bottom until you said yes to the missioner who married us. I can hear you giggle when you read this, but you were then too frightened to giggle. Admit it.

I shall be sending you messages through the Superintendent at Bourke, and if they are stiff in substance read my continuing love between the lines, between the words, and between every letter. You have been a sailor's wife for forty years, and to you I owe all that I have become.

Au revoir, Sweetheart,

Your devoted Bony.

Chapter Twenty-Five

Mrs Cosgrove Is Baffled

When Ray Cosgrove returned with the additional men, others filled up the last road-cut in the levee. These three stockmen were happy men, for they had been living lonely lives and they entered now a period of community life well worth the physical labour they were called to. They were unmercifully chaffed for having been brought off their horses to manhandle a shovel.

Bony borrowed a horse and rode with Ray down to the point opposite the Murrimundi homestead. Here both banks were high and the river raced with urgent speed. Ray fired the rifle he had brought to attract the attention of the homestead. A man appeared from among the cluster of date-palms shielding the house, and they could hear him shouting, although they were unable to distinguish the words. Another man joined him, and together they came to a high gum from which cables stretched to the one under which Bony and Ray waited.

The first man climbed a ladder with the blue mail-bag. He disappeared among the branches, and a moment later the second man began to turn a wheel and the [illegible]peared sitting on a sling and being drawn acr[illegible] the river.

Having descended to be greeted by Ray and introduced to Bony, his first question was, 'How's your flood coming?'

'Pretty good, John. How's yours?' replied Ray.

'Getting lusty.' He was perhaps thirty. The sun had so weathered his face that his complexion was darker than Bony's. 'Going to be a beaut this time. You're working on your levee, I bet.'

'Working! We're slaving on her. You're lucky.'

'Who have you got in off the track?' asked the other, and Ray listed them. 'You have some help, then. Lucas has been asking about what no-hopers we have. None at the moment, and don't need 'em.'

'Do many of them make camp at your old wool-scouring site?' Bony asked, and was told the place wasn't favoured, being off a direct line from one station kitchen to another.

'The last fellers to camp there were Miner Smith, and Champion, who you got now at Mira.'

'Smith says they were camped at the scour the day before Lush disappeared, the same day and day after. Have you any reason to doubt that?'

'Can't say I have. Any reason for Smith to lie about it?'

'He says, further, that during their stay they saw no other swagmen. I am now testing that. How far east from the opposite bank is the track on that side?'

'A couple of miles. You came down on it. I'll tell you what. I think the boss sent two men with a dray to get something at the scour that day Lush left his utility. I could find out from them who was there: if Smith is telling lies or not.'

'How fortunate! Do so, please. How soon can you let me have the information?'

'About fifteen minutes after I take your mail to the office. Well, see you later. Give my compliments to Jill, Ray, and tell her we're sorry about her mother, and hope like hell that the feller who bashed her will soon be caught.'

Winking at Bony, he climbed the ladder and soon was being drawn back over the river.

'What does he do?' Bony asked.

'Keeps the books. Runs the store. Murrimundi's six times larger than Mira, but it has a lot of useless land. You ever done accounting? I tried, but couldn't stand it.'

The youthful book-keeper appeared and eventually crossed again.

'I saw those fellers,' he said. 'They say they were loading with old iron about three in the afternoon when Champion and Miner Smith came from fishing in a hole up-river. It was the day Lush left his utility. Our fellers both say they saw no other swagmen and no signs of any others being there. I asked if they had gone into the old hut, and one said he had, and even Smith and his mate hadn't actually camped in it. So Smith must be speaking the truth.'

'Thank you very much,' Bony said warmly. 'Good of you to co-operate. It was just a little point I wanted to clear up.'

'No trouble, Inspector. Any time. Now I'll get back as the boss is in the office, and we all know what bosses are.'

Riding again, Bony was less depressed than he had been when writing to Marie, who, also being of the two races, was so close to him. When they were half-way home Ray asked whether he was getting places, and Bony gave him the same mysterious smile he had given Mrs Cosgrove.

Coming down-river they had crossed one of several shallow creeks which now, on the return to Mira, was running water from the river. The detour they were forced to take added several miles to the journey.

'Our place'll be surrounded by morning,' Ray predicted. 'There's a creek that's running uphill. It'll fill a depression four miles across before the water will run out again into the river. The old Dad used to talk about it. Looks as though the river will reach the office veranda, and a couple of million ducks will be swimming in through the door.'

'It was like that when the Paroo came down in flood. I was there,' Bony said.

The sun was setting beyond the Mira mail-box when they arrived at the office with the inward mail, and the sky promised windless days and cold nights. Bony was glad of the fire in MacCurdle's private room, and this evening he did not refuse the proffered drink.

'How are the men going, Mac?' asked Ray.

'Very well, I think, but not good enough for your mother.' The manager looked over the match held above his pipe. 'Times have changed, even here in Australia. No one works as hard and for as little as our grandfathers did. The way to handle a man in this situation isn't to tut-tut when he leans on a shovel to wait until the first critical moment and then raise his bonus. He'll work harder than his grandfather if he's paid high enough.'

'I agree, Mac, but mother is mother. What about

chaining her to a wall so she can't go out with the men?'

' 'Tis not a moment for facetiousness,' the Scotsman said, and Bony stepped into the breach.

'Permit me to approach Mrs Cosgrove. Now that could be Lucas wanting me.'

Ray, who took the call, said it was, and Lucas made his report.

'I talked to Petersen, Bony, and took the revolver from him. He made no fuss about it. It wasn't loaded, and I searched him and went through his swag for cartridges and found none. I asked why he carried the weapon, and he said just to frighten anyone, like a young feller who bailed him up a few years ago and robbed him. I told him he could have the gun back after I'd poured lead into the muzzle, and he said it wasn't any good anyway. It isn't either. The trigger mechanism's ruined. Seems he only carried it to frighten off attack.

'Well, he slept that night by the fire outside the Mira shed,' Lucas went on. 'He was anxious to start work at the Vospers' place and was on the move before sun-up. He saw no one about the homestead, but did see a man known as Bullocky Alec filling a bucket at the waterhole below The Brothers' camp. He crossed the river and instead of following the bank made direct for the mail-boxes through Madman's Bend.

'He was well into the bend when the sole of one of his old sandshoes came off, and he stopped to sew it on again with packing-needle and twine. He said he'd nearly finished the shoe when he heard a shot from the direction of the boxes. I went into this shot business, and he said it sounded like a twenty-two rifle, but adm⣿ ⣿at the wind was rising and could have reduced t⣿⣿ effect.

'When I got down to distance and time, he came out with the information that while on the job he thought he might as well attend to the other shoe, which was also in bad shape. He thinks he was about half-way through the bend when he heard the shot, that the second shoe occupied him half an hour, and it would be about half an hour to come out of the bend at the utility.'

'Did you test him on the likelihood of the shot having been fired at Madden's homestead?' asked Bony.

'Yes, and he seemed certain it came from the boxes. He put the time as seven-thirty. The wind strength would have prevented anyone at Mira hearing the report, and the noise in the trees at Madden's place would prevent anyone there from hearing it.'

'Seems logical, Lucas. Continue with Petersen.'

'According to Petersen there was no one in or near the ute. He didn't know who owned it, and said he wasn't interested. He cut across country to pick up the track from Madden's to Vospers', boiled his billy at a well called Blackman, and reached Vospers' in time to be given lunch.'

'Better obtain instructions from the Super about the disposal of the weapon, Lucas,' Bony said. 'And you might be able to fire it by thumbing the hammer. If so, get specimens of bullets, and hold them for checking. Thanks a lot. Oh, and check on the man called Bullocky Alec. It might not have been him Petersen thinks he saw.'

It was as Cosgrove predicted, for the following morning the water surrounded the homestead. During

the night the river had risen five feet and now the
trees bordering Madman's Bend appeared to be
absurdly stunted, and ashamed of it.

Bony accompanied MacCurdle, who drove a jeep
to inspect the work done on the levee. He stared at
the reddish water covering the flats behind the pro-
tected area. The track to the back end of the run,
the one by which he and Ray had gone for the mail,
and the road to Bourke, on this side, were all submerged; the nearest pieces of dry land were the
isolated salmon pink sand-dunes marking the verge
of the higher plain country.

The manager was sombre, and he grunted disapproval when he saw Mrs Cosgrove talking with
overseer Vickory in charge of a gang. This morning
she was wearing slacks and stockman's boots, and
when the jeep stopped she came to speak to Mac-
Curdle.

'Mac, I think the men are going slow purposely.
I simply don't understand it. I've told them I'll
double the bonus. If they won't work properly, then
the river will break through.'

'Perhaps the dignity of labour has something to
do with it,' Bony said quietly. 'All these men are here
because there is more than money attracting them.
Were it only money they would be living in a nice
coastal city. They choose to live in this outback for
the same reason that you have come to do. They have
been moulded by this outback, and when they pack
up and move on and on, it is because the movement,
bringing remembered scenes, also gives the assurance
of freedom from being compelled to obey a factory
whistle, to catch a train or bus on the minute, to
work, or sleep in a park and be harried by the police.'

Mrs Cosgrove regarded Bony as she had done when he landed from the trip across the river.

The manager said tartly, 'That's the truth of it, Mrs Cosgrove.'

'One thing, and quite important, too, that they dislike is being watched by a woman while working,' continued Bony. 'By going slow they are giving a hint. If you were not here they might well work normally, because again they differ from city workers, who watch the clock, and who work under the eye of a foreman. In the city, constant hostility between worker and boss: here there isn't that hostility.'

'You put it very well, Bony, and you make me inclined to accept the hint. It isn't the first time I find myself failing to understand you Australians. I'll go back to the house with you.'

'Wise woman,' Bony said, smilingly. 'And we shall be in time for morning smoko.'

'You Australians think of nothing more than tea-drinking, and you have ruined me as well.'

Bony spent the remainder of the morning, and part of the afternoon, telephoning the surrounding homesteads from Bourke down to Tilpa, below White Bend, and making additional notes on his map. There were disclosed fourteen men who had had opportunity to murder William Lush, and two of them were the most likely killers. In every case motive was lacking. The means could have been possessed by any one of them.

Chapter Twenty-Six

Bony and His Shovel

Bony borrowed old pants and boots and reported to
Vickory for work the following morning. He was
received by his work-mates with a derisive cheer, and
offered ten or a dozen shovels.

'This is goin' to be good,' declared the solemn man
in the torn coat. 'To see a flamin' detective on the
right end of a shovel is goin' to make me young all
over again.'

'Then you and the inspector can move on closer
to the 'dozer,' Vickory ordered, and the pair did as
directed. After twenty minutes of silent but steady
working Champion asked if Bony had been put on to
work for his tucker, and with a show of indignation
Bony said he wouldn't work for a squatter below
union wages.

'What's the bonus they're paying?' he countered.

'She raised it to half the wages this morning. Then
looked narked 'cos we went slow. Hate being gawped
at by a woman boss.'

Bony announced his agreement, and the following
conversation was spasmodic. They discussed the river
and the odds in favour of defeating it. Then Champion mentioned Lush and asked if Bony 'was doing
any good'.

'Stump   Champion. Couldn't pick up tracks before the river came down. By the way, where were you that day Lush vanished?'

'I was camped with a feller called Miner Smith at the old wool-scour on Murrimundi. You don't drag me into it.'

'Still, you've only his word about that, and he has only your own. Any backing?'

'No. No other travellers. But we got backing, if that's what you're looking for. That day the ute was found two blokes from the homestead came to load old iron. We was up-river, fishing, and they was there when we got back. Ask 'em.'

'I don't think I'll trouble. I'm beginning to make up my mind that it's Petersen I want. He was camped here the night before and he left very early to go out to Vospers' to work. I'm told he carries a .32 calibre revolver, and Lush was shot by a thirty-two. Now I'm stuck here, and where he'll be when I get away from this flood could be a thousand miles off. You might keep it dark from the others.'

'Too right!' agreed Champion, and Bony knew it would be passed round at the camp fire that night. 'How did you find out old Pete carries a gun?'

'He told me.'

'Told you? You goin' to get him put up for it?'

'Certainly not,' answered Bony. 'No business of mine until I pin this murder on him. I'm not nailing fellers for carrying a concealable weapon. That's the job for the New South police. I'm a Queensland detective. Didn't you know?'

'I didn't. But all you police are as thick as thieves, aren't you?'

'On many points, yes. On others, no. We have a

union, too. Stick to the rules like other unionists. We don't go around scabbing on the police in other States. Only on homicide jobs. My trouble's if every swagman on the Darling carries a gun. I've a wife to maintain.'

By afternoon smoko Bony was beginning to feel the strain of this unaccustomed labour, and long before knock-off time he was watching the sun. A hot shower revived his weary muscles, and he was feeling happy at having tested Miner Smith's statement that no other swagman turned up at the scour while he and Champion were there, and by having directed attention to Petersen.

Immediately after dinner he put on blackened tennis shoes, and replaced his collar with a black scarf; noting the direction of the light wind, he made his way in the dark to draw near enough to the swag-men's fire to listen in to the talk. He was not long there when Champion unconsciously played the part awarded him.

'The d. told me he's after Petersen. Said Petersen left here early that morning Lush got his, to work for Vospers. Reckons Lush was at the ute. He threatened Petersen and the old bloke shot him.'

'Wouldn't put it past him,' said Silas Wishart. 'Lush would'a been too good for him at his age.'

They discussed Petersen as the likely killer, and the majority found him innocent. Then someone pointed out that the police would be down on him, anyway, for carrying a revolver, and Champion took up this point, repeating Bony's aversion to breaking union rules. It was now that the old saying that eaves-droppers seldom hear good of themselves had some-thing to it.

'He's a funny sort of cop,' said thick-set Bosun Dean. 'Could be as he says. Them half-castes are pretty canny. Don't say much and don't give much away to the boss. He's down here on a murder case, so why should he poke his nose after blokes carrying a gun? I carry one meself, not having a mate to travel with.'

'I don't,' said the Paroo Bikeman. 'I'm in foul enough with the cops as it is. A well-ground dinner knife's good enough for me. But talking of half-castes being cocky with their bosses is about right. Give 'em a foot and they take a mile.'

Champion couldn't let his bone alone.

'Seemed pretty sure Petersen bumped Lush. He was moanin' that he got that way only late last night, and now the flood's cut him off from chasin' after him. I asked him how he was so certain, and he looked wise. Then I said it mightn't be old Petersen, and d'you know what? When I says it could of been someone in this camp he says he's sure the murderer ain't here 'cos he would've cleared out days ago, and no one's cleared out.'

'Good arguing,' said Mick the Warder. 'If I had finished Lush I wouldn't be here now, inspector or no inspector. I wouldn't be hanging about the scene of the crime.'

'You used to have a gun, Mick. Still got it?' asked a man known to Bony as Bill Wishart.

'I changed it for a forty-four Winchester. Musta been two years back. Bloke by the name of Teacher Miles. Ever see him up this way?'

'Heard about him,' said Wally Watts. 'Victorian, ain't he? Could use himself somewhat, someone told me.'

'That's him,' agreed Mick the Warder, and Dead March Harry said, 'The gun went off. Bomb . . . Bomb . . . Bomb . . .'

'Oh, cut it out, Harry,' complained Mick. 'You can't keep on going off the deep end, and the tablets are gettin' low. Here, you'd better take one now. I'll get the water.' The tall mournful man stood, and had repeated the solemn note twice when his mate brought the water, made him swallow the tablet and took him off to bed.

There followed prolonged silence. Champion broke it.

'Looks after him like he was 'is son. I don't think Harry's gettin' any worse, do you?'

The question was directed to Bosun Dean, but Silas Wishart took it up.

'Yes, he's gettin' worse. They was camped with us, and Harry took off four times in two days. Used to be more'n a week for one go. Time'll come when Mick will have to put him away. Mick knows it, too. Funny! I don't have time for warders any more than coppers, but I'd put my hat on Mick any day.'

'Yair, good poor bastard,' admitted the Paroo Bikeman, standing up. 'Well, here's me for the blankets. I've had it.' The Brothers said they had had it, too, and the four men departed into the night to cross to the shearers' quarters. Wally Watts stood up, stretched and sat again on the packing-case.

'The Brothers were talking about striking tomorrow. Whata you think about it?'

'Don't mind if I do,' answered Bosun Dean.

Champion voted the other way. 'Don't seem right,' he said. 'We're getting good pay.'

'It's the way I think,' Wally Watts said. 'We'll have

to vote on it, anyway, and I abide by the majority. I'm into the bunk. Good night!'

The others went with him, and Bony thoughtfully returned to join MacCurdle in the office.

'I believe tomorrow will see the climax, Mac. The wind has shifted to the north, and the stars are dim. D'you know what Macey said of today's chart?'

'That a low was approaching and a change predicted. The house radio said soon after you left this evening that the change should enter the State in forty-eight hours. As you said, if the wind blows hard from the west we might be up against it.'

'I'm turning in,' Bony said. 'Could be hard day coming.'

'No need for you to work on the levee. Appreciated, though.'

'Everyone will be wanted on that levee, Mac.'

Bony was up at daybreak, and was aghast at the sight of the water topping the bank verge and lying against the base of the levee. Where the flood rounded the bend the surface gently boiled, and the far line of gums was visibly lower in the water. After breakfast he went to work and found not a man on the job.

'They're holding a meeting,' the men's cook told him. 'Even Jacko's gone there.'

'Where are they holding the meeting?'

'In the shearing-shed. The station men are with them. So's the manager and Vickory, waiting to see how things will go.'

'What's your attitude?'

The cook's eyes gleamed, and the smile about his mouth was sour.

'They go on strike, I go on strike, and they don't eat. Fair enough, ain't it?'

222

Nodding agreement, Bony walked swiftly to the shed, where he found the overseer and the manager standing by the ash mound of the outside fire. They could hear a man speaking to the meeting. Bony nodded to them and entered the shed to stand at the rear of the assembled workers. Silas Wishart was saying, 'There it is, fellers, Mrs Cosgrove says she won't raise the bonus. We know that station hands' wages plus the bonus don't equal the wages of city workers. I reckons we strike until she raises the bonus to make the pay twice station hands' pay. It's hard enough labour and worth the dough.'

'All right, we'll take a vote on it,' said the Paroo Bikeman. 'If the vote's for strike, then the scabs had better look out.'

The threat of being labelled a scab would hold back every man who voted to work, should the majority vote to strike. Men looked at each other in an effort to see how the vote might go. Others betrayed nervousness. Bony, seeing a wool table close by, climbed to stand and address the startled men.

'If you decide to strike,' he began, blue eyes flashing, 'there must be inevitable results. You listen to what they will be. One is that the owner of Mira is a woman, and a very stubborn woman who declares she will not increase the bonus. The result of a strike will almost certainly be the smashing of the levee by the waves which will be raised by the rising west wind. That won't be so great a catastrophe as some of you think. Not for Mrs Cosgrove it won't, but by heck it will be for you!'

'How?' a man shouted.

'Get down, copper,' yelled another. Then Wally Watts spoke.

'Hold it! Let him have his say.'

'It's going to be just too bad for all of you should you go on strike at this particular time,' Bony continued. 'If the levee gives way, you know what will happen to the Mira homestead, and I'll tell you what will surely happen to all of you. You will be hunted off this river, and what will hunt you will be starvation, for no homestead will ever again give you a handout or sell any food to any of you. Your freedom will be gone, because you are free to walkabout when and wherever you wish. You can get away to the wheat cockies, or down to the cities, and there you have only the simple choice of working or starving.

'For decades it has been the custom for homesteads to give out rations so that when men are needed there will be men at hand. It's almost a law of the outback, and should you strike under the present circumstances you will be breaking one of the finest customs ever.'

Support came from a most unexpected quarter.

'Blast me if he ain't right! Anyone game to call me a scab?' inquired the Paroo Bikeman, with sinister mildness. He was supported by Wally Watts and Champion. The remainder followed without troubling to take a vote.

Chapter Twenty-Seven

Victory and Defeat

The wind from the north increased to become a stiff breeze, and its direction and speed were steady for the remainder of the day. Its effect on the levee facing the mile-long reach was negligible, but by evening the level of the river was two feet up from the base.

Mrs Cosgrove would have no cause to complain had she watched the workers today, but she discreetly kept out of sight. Jill Madden had early insisted on relieving the station groom of milking the few cows, then of shepherding the ration sheep for the scant herbage and, towards evening, of slaughtering three of them. MacCurdle grabbed a shovel and joined Bony and Champion with Silas Wishart and his two brothers. It was shortly after eight the next morning when the wind moved to the west and began to work up to a gale.

By midday the position was alarming. The eye of the wind continued steadfastly at the two distant mail-boxes. It produced short waves about thirty inches high to beat upon the levee, and created a false average level as the water swirled round the bend like a highway built higher at the outside than the inside of a sharp angle.

No longer did men lean on their shovels; no longer

were there periodic pauses by the machines; for now there was no hostility between capital and labour; they were united against a common enemy. The river had become a personality to be fought, and subdued if humanly possible.

During the latter part of the afternoon the men were so absorbed by the struggle that only Bony noticed Dead March Harry drop his shovel, straighten up, and begin to walk away with his measured tread. Mick the Warder was working several hundred yards away, and Bony could see that he was unaware of his mate's latest turn.

Bony went after Harry and gripped him by the arm. His intention was to keep the man out of danger and to steer him back to Mick. Above the wind in the trees he could hear the bomb-bomb-bombing, and then the repeated phrase 'I'm dead.'

'You're not, Harry. You're all right now. Let us go this way.'

'Dead! The gun went off. It wasn't his fault. The bastard threatened to have me put away. Dead! I'm dead! Bomb! Bomb! Bomb!'

They were proceeding towards the levee when Mick the Warder saw them and came running. His face vividly expressed his concern. He caught hold of Harry's other arm and said, 'Thanks, Inspector. I didn't see him leaving. What a time to have another turn! Come on, Harry, old feller. It's you for a tablet and a lie down for a bit.'

Bony went back to work with Harry's tragedy riding him, and Mick's concern arousing pity and humbleness. Then there was no time for anything but shovelling, and tramping, and being constantly half-blinded by spray.

The sun went down, and with it the wind. At six o'clock not a wave broke, the surface of the now sullen river pressing against the levee, and the tired men at dinner spoke barely a word.

MacCurdle appeared and from the head of the long table said, 'As from this morning the bonus will be doubled, and will be continued until the danger to the levee has passed. I hope that if needed during the night you'll turn out. Thanks.'

Three nights and two days passed before the river began to fall. Both the manager and Bony were exhausted. They had worked night shifts patrolling the levee with a lamp and a shovel. During this period Bony was engaged in a spiritual battle, and at the end of it he was as exhausted mentally as he was physically.

Having seen the evidence of the river drop against the levee, he returned to the office and rang Superintendent Macey.

'Ah there, Bony the Rebel!' said Macey. 'How's the flood? How's the levee?'

'The flood is going down and the levee is safe.' Bony made sure no one was present, and softly went on, 'I want to make an arrest, to hold on suspicion. I have proven opportunity. I have proven motive. But I haven't as yet proven means. I want assistance.'

'Very well, I'll send the assistance, probably this afternoon.'

'Make it as soon as possible, Superintendent. The situation I find myself in must be controlled by accurate timing.'

'That will be kept in mind. What do you suggest?'

Bony outlined his plan, and Macey accepted it.

· · · · ·

At three o'clock the men's cook smote his iron triangle, and at three-five all the men were at table. At three-fifteen Ray Cosgrove drove a utility to the airstrip. Ten minutes later a light aircraft landed, and two hard-faced men alighted and were driven to meet Mick the Warder and his pathetic mate.

'Michael Carmody, I have a warrant to arrest you on suspicion of having murdered William Lush on July 19 this year,' one said. 'You may want to collect your dunnage. We have no authority over a man called Dead March Harry, but have been instructed to tell you he may accompany us to Bourke where he will receive medical attention. You going to co-operate or—?'

'You can keep your handcuffs,' answered Mick the Warder. 'Come on, Harry.'

He strode on in the direction of the shearers' quarters, leaving Dead March Harry to walk between the policemen, but he dropped back on seeing Bony and MacCurdle standing outside the door.

'Sir,' said one of the strangers from Bourke, 'we have made the arrest. The prisoner wishes to collect his belongings.'

Bony unlocked the door. On either side of the central passage of the long building were the two-man cubicles, and Bony asked which was occupied by Mick the Warder and his mate. The room was pointed out, and the six men became a crowd within it.

'Which is your bed, Mick?' asked Bony, and the man indicated it.

Only the straw mattress and bedstead belonged to the station. Bony went through the coverings, raised the mattress, disclosed the revolver, and sighed. With it was a small hide bag containing cartridges. It was handed to one of the visiting policemen, who noted the serial number in his book, broke it open, found it unloaded, and sighted down the barrel against a thumb-nail. The manager, too, was asked to note the number.

'Have you anything to say, Mick?' Bony asked.

'You planted the gun, Inspector.'

'I didn't know which room you have been occupying. I have never been inside this building. There is every reason to suspect that this weapon was fired at William Lush. You will know that proof or otherwise will be easily obtained. Would you care to tell us why you shot Lush?'

'You outline your case, first.'

'Very well, I'll do that because you have to make up your mind what is to become of Harry. Even I am concerned on that point. To begin, I asked you where you were on the night of July 18–19, and you said you were camped with Harry at the old wool-scour up-river from Murrimundi· homestead. You were not. Champion and Miner Smith were, and they did not see either of you. Also, two Murrimundi men visited the place and found no evidence of your being there.

'On July 17 you called at Madden's Selection for a handout. Then you went down-river and camped with The Brothers. Early on the morning of the nineteenth you left The Brothers and went up-river, with what purpose I don't know, and it isn't important. You saw Lush's utility stalled at the mail-boxes, and either found Lush there or were found there by him. An argument developed, and Lush threatened to have Harry put away. You realized he was in the squatter class, while you were swagmen, and that he could make good his threat. So you shot him and heaved his body over and into the water-hole.

'Then you portioned between you the bottles of liquor in the carton, and retreated into Madman's Bend, where you camped awhile to plan what you would do, and also to open one of the bottles of whisky. From there I haven't been able to trace you, but you kept out of sight until the morning you were seen by the mail driver. That was several miles south of the Mira–Madden boxes, and you were walking northward. You staged that meeting because every-one here knows that swagmen travel great distances up and then down, and vice versa, and it would be natural for him and others to believe you had been many miles south of the boxes when Lush vanished.'

'Not bad, Inspector,' Mick conceded. 'Give us some more.'

'I'll oblige, Mick. There is a man named Petersen. On the morning of the nineteenth he was boiling his billy at the shed fireplace when he saw a man descend from The Brothers' camp to the hole below it and there fill a bucket. His eyesight isn't good, but he was sure it was a man known as Bullocky Alec. He was wrong, for Bullocky Alec was in the Wil-cannia lock-up that day. It was you who drew water from the hole, and you strongly resemble Bullocky Alec. An easy mistake to make for a man with poor sight, and in view of the distance between the shed and the hole below The Brothers' camp. It's quite a minor point.'

'You're telling me,' agreed Mick. 'Old Petersen carries a revolver. He must have passed Lush's ute on his way to Vospers' that morning. Dig into him.'

'We have,' Bony said. 'Now if only you had rid yourself of the revolver just found under your mattress.'

Mick the Warder sat on the bed beside Dead March Harry, who was staring at the floor. He gripped his mate's arm, and said, softly pleading, 'Harry, did you tell about Lush's threat to have you sent away? You must have done. There was no one else there bar you and me.'

Dead March Harry raised his face to look at Mick the Warder.

'I don't remember, Mick,' he said, and Bony could see the struggle in his eyes. 'Must have done. I remember Lush rushing us and shouting we were stealin' his booze. Mad as a snake. Tore off a box leg and aimed at me. Hurt my shoulder he did. Yelled he'd have me put away, and swiped again and missed and hit his ute. The gun went off. The gun went off. The gun . . .'

It was Harry who terminated the ensuing silence. He stood and lifted a foot, and from him issued the familiar 'Bomb!'

'That's torn it,' Mick said, and sighed. 'Yes, if only I'd ditched the gun. Give him a tablet. Here, in this bottle.' Mechanically, Harry accepted the tablet from Bony. 'It was as he says. We went there to fish and saw the ute and was eyeing it over when Lush come from nowhere. He rushed Harry with the box leg, and hit him, and Harry stood still and would have got it again. I couldn't get round the ute in time to stop it. I don't think Lush even saw me, he was that mad. I had to drop him with a bullet. And there wasn't any grog to pinch. Lush musta hid it. I wouldn't have taken a bottle, anyway, because grog's no good for Harry. Inspector, will you see he gets a fair go?'

'You can be very sure about that, Mick. Very, very sure.'

'I'm dead,' declared Dead March Harry.

'Dead be damned!' Mick told him and shook him. 'Come on now, and pack up. We're going to town for a spell. Just a little spell, and then we'll come back to the Gutter. Bet cher!'